D1101128

This book should be returned to any branch of the
Lancashire County Library on or before the date shown

MR RIGHT,
NEXT DOOR!

MR RIGHT, NEXT DOOR!

BY

BARBARA WALLACE

First published in Great Britain 2012
by Mills & Boon, an imprint of Harlequin (UK) Limited.
Large Print edition 2012
Harlequin (UK) Limited, Eton House,
18-24 Paradise Road, Richmond, Surrey TW9 1SR

© Barbara Wallace 2012

ISBN: 978 0 263 22634 8

2/13

11811233 7

Printed and bound in Great Britain
by CPI Antony Rowe, Chippenham, Wiltshire

For Pete, my own special contractor.
I can't imagine life without you.

CHAPTER ONE

HE WAS doing it again.

Since she'd moved in a month ago, Sophie Messina's neighbor had been banging, buzzing and doing Lord knows what in his upstairs apartment, making it completely impossible for her to concentrate.

Didn't he realize some people liked quiet on their weekends? That people had work to do?

Breathing out a determined sigh, she redoubled her efforts. Allen Breckinridge, one of her managing directors, had announced yesterday afternoon that he needed this merger model for a meeting on Tuesday, which meant she needed to review and correct the work her junior analyst sent over this morning before passing the figures along. And, since no report could ever be finalized without repeating the process at least four times, she needed to make her notes quickly. A lot of analysts would be tempted to make nit-picky comments, more to emphasize their involvement than anything, but Sophie preferred to work efficiently. Last thing she wanted was the managing directors thinking she was the kink in the bottleneck. Especially since she planned on being a managing director herself someday. Sooner rather than later too if all went according to plan.

Bam!

Oh, for crying out loud, what was he doing up there? Kickboxing holes in the wall? She whipped off her reading glasses and tossed them on the dining room table. This was ridiculous. She must have slipped a half-dozen notes under his door asking him to kindly cease and desist whatever it was he was doing. First politely, and then threatening to bring the issue to the co-op owners association, but he'd ignored all of them. Well, no more. This noise was going to stop. Today.

Smoothing back her sleek blond ponytail, she stepped outside into the building entryway and shivered as her bare feet met the wood flooring. Before being renovated into co-op apartments, the building had been a brownstone mansion. For one reason or another, the architects kept the public areas and her apartment as true to the original decor as possible which was why a large and very ornate crystal chandelier hung in the entranceway. Sophie had to admit, she loved everything about the nineteenth-century fixtures, from the dark wood molding to the sprawling central stairway with its spindled railings and balustrade. They gave the building an Old World kind of feeling, conjuring up words like *historic* in her head. Words that implied stability. She liked stability.

She liked tranquility, too. A quality that had been distinctly absent the past four weekends. As she climbed the stairs, she swore the banging grew louder with each step. Did he have to do whatever it was he was doing at the loudest possible volume?

This wasn't how she envisioned her first conversation with a neighbor. Actually, she hadn't planned on having a conversation at all. One of the reasons she moved to the city two decades ago was because you could go months, years even, without exchanging more than a nod and a hello with the people around you. Not that she was antisocial. She just preferred being able to choose who she socialized with. She had too much she needed to accomplish to waste time frivolously. The only reason she even remotely knew this particular neighbor's name was because his mailbox was located next to hers, and she'd needed to know who she should address her letters to. G. Templeton. She'd seen the same name on the side of a pickup truck parked outside. Some sort of contractor, she believed.

Was that what he was doing now? Contracting? Memories of half-finished DIY projects and drunken destruction popped into her brain before she could stop them. What the heck? Buying her own place was supposed to distance her from those days, not bring them racing back. At her age she should be over being plagued by the ghosts of the past. Yet no matter how much she accomplished or worked, they never seemed to completely recede. She could always feel them, lurking, keeping her on guard. In some ways, their insistence was a blessing; they kept her working and focused. Otherwise, she'd still be stuck in some banged-up, roach-infested apartment like the one she grew up in on Pond Street, instead of owning her own brownstone co-op. A co-op she'd thought would be quiet and tranquil.

By the time she reached the second floor landing, noise punctuating each step, Sophie was thoroughly aggravated. Every bang seemed to reverberate off the fleur-de-lis wallpaper and settle right between her shoulder blades fueling her irritability. Mr. Templeton was going to get an earful, that's for certain. Summoning up every inch of her authoritative demeanor, she knocked on his door. The response was another bang.

Fine. Two could play this game. She pounded back in kind.

"Mr. Templeton," she called sharply.

"Hold on, hold on, I'm coming!" a gruff voice called out. As if *he* were the one being bothered.

Folding her arms across her chest, Sophie prepared to remind Mr. Templeton about the existence of other residents and the need to respect people's personal solitude, not to mention their right to an undisturbed weekend.

The door opened.

Good God Almighty. Sophie's biting lecture died on her tongue. Standing on the other side of the threshold had to be, hands-down, the most incredible-looking man she'd ever seen. Not cover-model handsome—*handsome* was far too benign a word anyway—but rugged in a sensual way with smooth tanned skin and a square-cut jaw. A slightly too-long nose kept his face from being overly perfect and yet on him the feature fit. Strong men demanded strong features and this, Sophie could tell, was definitely a strong man. He had hair the color of dark honey and eyes that reminded her of caramel candy. Not to mention a chest custom-built for splaying your hands against.

He was also at least a decade younger than she was, and holding a sledgehammer, the obvious source of her disturbance. Both realizations quickly brought Sophie back to earth. She lifted her jaw, once again prepared to complain.

"Mr. Templeton?" she repeated. Just to be certain.

The caramel eyes made a slow sweep of her from head to toe. "Who wants to know?"

If he thought the open assessment would unnerve her, he was mistaken. She'd been fending off harassing looks since college graduation. None of them as blatant or as smoldering perhaps, but she'd fended them off nonetheless. "I'm Sophie Messina from downstairs."

He nodded in recognition. "The lady who writes the notes. What can I do for you, Mrs. Messina?"

"Miss," she corrected, although she wasn't quite sure why, or why she didn't say "Ms."

Biceps rippled as he propped the hammer against the frame and folded his arms, mimicking her stance. "Okay, what can I do for you, Miss Messina?"

Sophie was pretty certain he already knew. "You've been doing a lot of banging lately."

"Renovating," he replied. "I'm gutting the main bathroom, getting her ready to install a claw-foot tub."

"Interesting." The image momentarily distracted her. Rough and rugged didn't go with claw-footed baths.

She smoothed her hair, as much to rein in her thoughts as to keep the unruly strands in line. "Well, I'm trying to build a financial model for a potential acquisition."

He drew his lips together. They were nice-shaped lips, too. "Financial model, did you say?"

"Yes. I'm an investment analyst. For Twamley Greenwood," she added, figuring the prestigious name might emphasize the project's significance.

"Good for you." Clearly, her employer credentials didn't impress him. "What would you like me to do?"

Wasn't the request obvious? Stop making so much blasted noise. "I wonder if you wouldn't mind keeping it down. Your loud banging makes concentrating difficult."

"Little hard to bang any softer," he drawled in reply. "By nature banging is a loud activity. Even the word—*bang*—" he let the word burst loudly from his lips "—implies as much."

Sophie gritted her teeth. She knew that condescending tone. He wasn't taking her complaint seriously. "Look," she said, drawing herself up to her full five feet and five inches—a meaningless gesture since he still had at least a half a foot on her. "I've asked you several times if you could please keep the noise down."

"No, you've slid notes under my door commanding me to 'cease and desist.' You haven't *asked* me anything."

"Fine. I'm asking you now. Could you please keep the noise down?"

"Sorry." He shook his head. "No can do."

No? "No?" she repeated.

"Told you, I'm gutting the bathroom. Do you have any idea what that entails?"

"Yes," she replied. Visions of those biceps swinging a sledgehammer came to mind.

"You sure? Because if you don't—" a gleam entered his brown gaze "—you're welcome to come in for a demonstration. Maybe even do a little swinging yourself."

"I—I—" Was he *flirting* with her? The audacity had her speechless. The image of those muscular arms didn't help, either.

Taking a deep breath, more to regain her mental purchase than anything else, she tried again. Blunter this time. "Look, Mr. Templeton, I have a lot of work to do—"

"So do I," he interrupted. He shifted his weight again, biceps rippling a little more. Challenging her or trying to distract her, Sophie wasn't sure. He was succeeding in doing both. "It's Saturday afternoon, not the middle of the night, and last time I looked, renovating *my* home, on *my* weekend, was completely acceptable. If the banging bothers you so much, I suggest you go build your model somewhere else."

That wasn't the point. Sure, she had a nice big office in the financial district where she could work, but Sophie didn't want to go into Manhattan. What good was owning your own home if you had to twist your life around others' wishes, and besides, she shelled out a lot of hard-earned money for this place. If she wanted to work at home, by God, she should be able to.

Which begged the question of how a guy his age managed to buy into this address in the first place. It had taken her twenty years of saving and paying off her education loans before she accumulated a sizable down payment. Maybe he didn't mind having debt the way she did. Or he was a closet millionaire. But then why would he be redoing his apartment by himself on weekends?

Never mind; she didn't really care. She just wanted to get back to work. "I would agree with you if we were talking about one afternoon, but we're talking every afternoon for a month. That's a lot of gutting."

"What can I say?" he answered with a shrug. "I've got a lot of renovation to do."

He was purposely ignoring her point. Sophie couldn't help noting her analysts would never get away with copping such an attitude. Maybe this confrontation would go better if she'd approached him when dressed more professionally. She'd be the first to admit her cotton skirt and Polo shirt didn't scream authority. Casual clothes tended to make her look girlish.

Still, she tried, jutting her chin and mustering her sternest voice. A take-no-excuses tone she'd perfected over the years. "What about the other tenants? How do they feel about all these renovations?"

He shrugged again. "No one's complained so far."

"Really?"

"You're the only one."

Sophie smoothed her ponytail. Time to make him take her complaints seriously; show him she meant business. "Perhaps when I bring this up to the building association you'll hear differently."

"Oh, right. I forgot your last note threatened to contact the association."

At last, maybe they were getting somewhere. "Glad to see you read them. I'm sure you'd prefer not to make this a big, official issue."

"I would, except for one thing." The gleam reappeared in his eye. "I'm the association president."

He had to be kidding.

"The other tenants didn't want to be bothered with building maintenance issues so they gladly let me handle everything," he continued. He unfolded his arms, jamming one hand in his back pocket and letting the other rest off the hammer handle. "Come to think of it, that's probably why they don't mind the banging."

"Unbelievable," Sophie muttered.

"Not really. Not when I'm the best person for the job. Now if you'll excuse me, I've got some tiles I need to take down." He reached for the door.

"Wait!" She shoved her bare foot forward to block the door. Thankfully he noticed. "What about the banging? What am I supposed to do until you're finished?"

"The store around the corner sells noise-canceling headphones. If I were you, I'd consider checking them out."

Sophie barely had time to slide her foot back before the door slammed in her face.

Five o'clock came early, and it came even earlier on Monday morning. Earlier still since Sophie had spent until almost 1:00 a.m. making sure the last round of revisions were done and in Breckinridge's in-box before going to bed. Much as she longed to sleep in and make up for the late hours, she couldn't. The overseas markets were already entering their volatile hours and she was expected to know what was going on. That is, she expected it of herself. She didn't want to risk the chance she'd get caught off guard. Being prepared was something she prided herself on, like being efficient and goal-oriented. Although all three would be a lot easier with more than four hours' sleep.

Then again, a lack of sleep came with the territory. If you wanted to get ahead, you put in the hours.

And, she intended to get ahead. So far ahead that eventually Pond Street and all the other ghosts from her past were nothing more than vague, faded images. Then once she'd made it, she'd retire early and sleep in all the mornings she wanted. She was already halfway along her timetable and if the rumors were true and Raymond Twamley was planning to step aside, she could be even closer. A full two years ahead of her schedule.

Until then, she'd always have coffee. She flipped off the plastic lid to see how much of the lifesaving liquid she had left. A quarter of caramel-colored liquid greeted her. Interesting, she thought. Her neighbor's eyes had been a similar color, especially when they'd taken on that flirtatious gleam. Not that she cared. The man had shut his door in her face, the hot-looking, rude…

"Reading tea leaves?"

She didn't have to look up to know who was asking. While normally she made a point of maintaining a professional distance from her colleagues, David Harrington was the one exception. A member of the firm's legal department, he had introduced himself at the company Christmas party a few years earlier, and she'd quickly discovered he made the perfect companion. "More like trying to see if I could absorb the caffeine through my eyeballs," she muttered.

A slight frown crossed his rangy features. "That's obviously not going to happen."

No kidding, Sophie almost said aloud, before quickly biting the words back. Normally she found David's tendency to be painstakingly literal easy to deal with, but lack of sleep had her tired and quick-tempered. It was going to take a lot of caffeine to keep her pleasant and reasonable all day.

Proving her point to herself, she took a long drink from her cup.

The silver-haired lawyer settled himself on the edge of the desk. Despite the early hour, he looked perfectly put together in his gray suit and aquamarine tie. But then, he always looked put together. He didn't have to try to look professional; he simply was.

"I stopped by to see how you were doing. You sounded pretty stressed when you cancelled our dinner date Saturday," he explained.

Sophie felt a little stab of guilt. "I am sorry about that," she replied. "Allen had the whole office running in circles all weekend. I barely had time to breathe."

He waved off her apology. "Forget it. I know all about Allen's demands. We'll try that particular restaurant another time."

"Thank you for understanding." One of the things she appreciated about David was that he *did* understand these things. He was also unflappable, professional and career-focused. *Uncomplicated.* That was the best word for him. True, he wasn't the most thrilling man in the

world and the physical aspects of their relationship wouldn't inspire love songs, but he was exactly the kind of man she would choose if and
when it came time to think about a long-term
relationship.

"I would have been lousy company even without Allen's last-minute project," she told him. "I
was having neighbor problems. Remember the
banger?" Briefly she filled him in on her encoun-
ter with G. Templeton, starting with the banging
and ending with their abrupt goodbye. For obvious reasons, she left out the part about his biceps
and flirtatious grin.

As she expected, David was appropriately
outraged. "He just shut the door in your face?
Without saying goodbye?"

"Clearly he felt he'd said all there was to say."

"More like he wanted to avoid the discussion.
I'm guessing you weren't the first neighbor to
complain."

"He says I am."

"Nonsense. Bet you ten dollars when the tenant
association meets, there are lots of complaints."

"Doubtful. Turns out he's the head of the association. The other residents didn't want the hassle," she added when David's eyes widened.

Picking up her discarded coffee lid, she twirled the plastic circle between her fingers. "Looks like I'm stuck listening to the banging until he finishes his project."

"What exactly is he doing anyway?"

She shrugged. "This week? Gutting his bathroom." To install a claw-foot tub. She couldn't get that particular image out of her head any more than she could erase the picture of his biceps flexing as he swung the sledgehammer.

Quickly she slapped the lid on her cup. "Whatever he was doing, the noise kept up the rest of the afternoon," she told David. "Then on Sunday, he spent the day hauling away the debris—" which sounded suspiciously like bags of cement blocks "—making sure he set them down as loudly as possible outside my door." Every time Sophie had heard the noise, she'd been jerked from her thoughts and swore he was doing so on purpose.

"Poor baby. No wonder you were aggravated.

You should have said something when I called. You could have come to my place."

"I'll keep that in mind for next time," Sophie replied, knowing she wouldn't. Why was everyone so eager for her to go somewhere else? Why couldn't they understand that she wanted to spend her weekends in her own home? Besides, hers and David's relationship worked perfectly the way it was. She wasn't ready to complicate matters by spending weekends together.

"In the meantime," she said, raising her cup to her lips, "thanks to spending the weekend on Allen's project, I'm behind on everything else."

"Including this morning's status report?"

Ignoring the fact he was interrupting their conversation, Allen Breckinridge strolled into her office. Sophie swallowed her mouthful of coffee. Naturally the managing director would arrive at the exact moment she mentioned being behind. The man had an uncanny knack for arriving at exactly the wrong time. Made her forever jumpy.

"Good morning, Allen," David greeted brightly. He was never jumpy. "Did you have a good weekend?"

"Good enough. Jocelyn and I spent it at the Hamptons," Allen replied. "About that progress report…"

"Right here," Sophie replied, shuffling through her papers for a hard copy. No sense pointing out that she had emailed a version to his computer last night; *I'm not at my computer,* he would say.

"Thank you," he said. He took the report while shooting David a look.

"I was just on my way out." The lawyer rose to his feet. "If you need any more information regarding that due diligence research, Sophie, let me know."

"I will." Silently, she added a "thank you." Another point in David's favor: his discretion. When it came to their outside relationship, he understood her desire to maintain a low profile.

Meanwhile, Allen was skimming the figures Sophie just handed him. Irrationally—because she'd double- and triple-checked the numbers— Sophie held her breath. There was an edge to the man's demeanor that made her perpetually worry she'd screwed up. To compensate for her nervousness, she fished through her papers again. "I also have the revised model figures you asked for."

"Never mind that." He tossed the report on her desk as though it were a meaningless memo. "I have a new project for you. Franklin Technologies is planning an IPO. I need an analysis for my meeting in Boston tomorrow morning."

"Of course. No problem." She and her staff could pull together a couple days' worth of research in a few hours.

And so began another typical Monday. She was going to need a whole lot of coffee.

Turns out, coffee wasn't enough. From the second Allen walked out of her office, Sophie found herself rushing around like a headless chicken, without about as much sense of direction, too. Every time she turned around someone needed something else, and she was asked to be the go-to girl. She missed lunch and dinner. Come to think of it, she decided while wolfing down a protein bar and a couple aspirin, having her head cut off might be preferable. At least then her neck might not be so stiff.

Finally she broke away for her nightly run thinking the endorphins might improve her mood. Wrong. All the forty-minute treadmill simulation did was add hot and sweaty to her already gigantic list of complaints. What the heck happened to the air-conditioning in the club anyway?

"Hey, where you heading?" someone hollered out as she made her way through the locker room to the showers. "Didn't you see the sign? The showers are closed."

What? Sure enough, a sign hung next to the door advising patrons that the club would be painting the showers and therefore shutting down the facilities early for one evening. "We apologize for the inconvenience," the note chirped at the bottom.

Her head sagged. Fat good an apology did her. She was a sweaty, frizzy-haired mess who still had several hours of work ahead of her when she got home.

And of course, since she was eager to get home, the trains weren't running on schedule. Meaning the crowd waiting just grew larger and larger so that when a subway car finally did arrive, she was forced to stand pressed into a horde of commuters as ripe and sweaty as she was. Naturally, the air-conditioning didn't work on the subway, either. And did the guy standing behind her, the one with all the shopping bags, really need to bump into her backside every time they lurched to a stop? *Lurch, bump. Lurch, bump.* No way was that a French baguette in his bag.

By the time she reached her front door, all Sophie could think about was stripping off her clothes and dousing herself with water. Maybe disinfectant, too, she added, thinking about shopping-bag man with a shudder. The water didn't even need to be hot. So long as she got clean.

Sliding her key into the front door was a little like greeting a long lost friend. *Home.* David and others, they could never truly understand the pleasure the word gave her. Or why she was so stubborn about spending her weekend here. That's because they'd been coming "home" their entire lives. They'd grown up in homes with normal parents and permanent addresses. For her, the term was still a novelty. True, since graduating college, she'd had apartments, luxury apartments in fact. Some in far better neighborhoods. But none had been hers. The day she signed her name to the mortgage, she'd achieved a goal she'd had since she was a teenager. She owned her own home. No more checks to landlords, no more temporary locations she could decorate but never really lay claim to. She could paint the living room neon green and it wouldn't matter because the place was *hers.*

With a welcome sigh, she tossed her gym bag on the bed and made her way to the shower. White-and-green tile greeted her when she switched on the light. When she bought the co-op the Realtor told her the previous owner insisted on keeping the original fixtures so, like the entranceway, the apartment had a very Old World, nineteenth-century look. David, of course, thought she should completely modernize the place and give it a sleeker look, but Sophie wasn't so sure. She'd clipped out a few sample photos from design magazines but nothing had truly captured her eye yet. Part of her liked the Old World feel. Again, it was that feeling of permanency. Knowing the building withstood the test of time. Kind of like her.

Then again, if she were using herself as a metaphor, modernizing made sense, too. A statement to the world that Sophie Messina had finally and truly arrived and was in control of her own destiny. Either way, she wasn't in a rush. She much preferred to take her time and develop a plan.

Right now, she'd take a hose and spray handle if it meant getting a shower. She reached past her green plaid shower curtain and turned the faucet handle.

Nothing came out.

Frowning, she tried the other hand. Again, nothing.

No way. This couldn't be happening. She checked the other faucets, including the small guest bath next to her second bedroom. All dry. Someone had shut off the water supply.

No, no, no! This couldn't be happening. An overwhelming need to pout and stomp her feet bubbled up inside her. Where was her water? Had she missed a notice about work here, too?

Just to be certain, she peeked outside to see if a note had been stuck to her front door. Nothing.

The pouting urge rose again. Of all the days to suffer her first home-owner problem. Why couldn't the water wait until tomorrow to fail? Or better yet, this past weekend.

Weekend. Of course! As the realization hit her, Sophie did stomp—all the way to her front door. She knew exactly what happened. And it involved a claw-foot bathtub.

CHAPTER TWO

"WHAT do you mean you said no?"

Grant ignored the incredulous tone of his brother, Mike, opting instead for taking a swig of beer. On the wall, the latest edition of the Boston–New York baseball rivalry played out in high definition. That's where he focused his attention. As far as Mike was concerned, he knew what was coming next.

"What heinous sin did the potential client commit this time? Choose the wrong paint color?"

Predictable as ever. "He wanted to go modern."

"Oh, well that explains everything. God forbid someone might like contemporary design."

"It was an original Feldman. Do you have any idea how rare those buildings are?" Scratch that. His brother had no idea. "There's maybe a handful of them left and this guy wanted to gut the place and turn it into two-bedroom condos."

"Better have him rung up on charges then. He's obviously committing a crime against humanity." Neither of them mentioned the fact that not so long ago, Grant would have committed the exact same crime.

"I hate to remind you, little brother, but there are people in this world who actually like living in buildings designed for the twenty-first century."

Grant didn't need reminding. "Then let them move into one built in the last twenty or thirty years, not rip apart an Art Deco gemstone."

"Says the man ripping up his own apartment."

"I'm not ripping apart anything, I'm righting a wrong." In more ways than one. He raised the bottle to his lips. "Somewhere my historical architecture professor is pulling out his hair."

"Give him a call, you two can ride off into the sunset on your matching high horses."

Talk about the pot calling the kettle black. Mike had been born on a high horse. "Since when is having principles a bad thing?" So what if he developed them a little late? He had them now.

"There's principles and then there's cutting off

your nose to spite your face. Sooner or later this attitude of yours is going to rear back and bite you in the ass."

Couldn't be worse than the injuries his old attitude caused. "Least then I'll be symmetrical."

Mike's sigh could be heard in New Jersey. "Seriously, you can't keep turning jobs down. Not if you want to build a successful business."

Ah yes, success. The Templeton family mantra. Settle for nothing less than the top. Grant knew it well. Hell, for the first twenty-seven years of his life he'd embodied it. Better than his older brother even.

"Maybe I'm not looking for my business to grow," he replied.

From the way his brother huffed, he might as well have suggested running naked through Central Park. "How about survive then? Did you miss the part of economics class where they explained you needed to have an income?"

"I didn't take economics." And he had income. Investment income, anyway. Enough to survive a good long dry spell as his brother knew perfectly well. "Another job will turn up. One always does."

"You hope. One of these days there won't be a job floating around. Then what? You're not going to be able to rely on that boyish charm of yours forever."

"Why not? Served me well so far." Though he preferred to use it for more personal transactions these days. Seduction was so much more pleasant without business attached. Less weight on the conscience.

"You need to think about the future, Grant."

Meaning he should get back on the corporate ladder where he belonged.

On television, the Boston first baseman watched a ball bound in front of home plate. Grant took a sip of beer in disgust, though whether it was over the team's million-dollar-arm's lousy performance or Mike's lecture was up for debate. No matter how many times he tried to get his family to understand, they just kept pitching. They thought he was wasting his education. Drifting. *Wallowing.*

"Do you and Dad draw straws to see who gets

this week's 'straighten Grant out' phone call?" Grant asked. "I haven't talked to Nicole in a while, maybe she'd like a shot, too, in between surgical rounds."

"We're concerned about you is all. You used to be so focused."

No, he'd been a tunnel-visioned tool. Why couldn't they see that he couldn't go back to being that man? Not and live with himself. Just thinking about those days made him sick to his stomach. He took another swig to wash away the bile.

"It's been two years," Mike said in a quiet voice.

"Two years, four months," Grant corrected. Did Mike really think that because some time had gone by, Grant would simply spring back to form? Nate Silverman wasn't springing anywhere, and Grant wouldn't, either, thanks to his self-centeredness.

"Nate would want—"

"Don't," Grant snapped. "Just don't." They both knew what Nate would want, and it had nothing to do with Grant or his future.

This time the bile couldn't be washed away. It never would be completely.

You were his best friend, Grant. How could you not see something was wrong? He called you for God's sake.

And Grant didn't take the call.

He squeezed his eyes shut. "Can we change the subject? Please?" The accusation haunted him enough. He didn't want to go there right now.

To his credit, Mike relented. Even he knew when to back off. "Sure. For now."

"Thank you."

"But you can't avoid the subject forever."

No kidding. His family wouldn't let him. "Did I tell you I met my new neighbor the other day?" Speaking of workaholics.

"The one who's been slipping notes under your door."

"In the flesh."

"What's she like?" Mike's voice took on a wincing tone. "Or is it a guy?"

"No, she's a woman, and she's exactly what you'd expect from a woman who uses phrases like 'cease and desist.'"

"I use that phrase."

"Precisely." Both his neighbor and his brother were high-end and tightly wound, only the neighbor was better looking. Grant could still picture her, all blonde and bossy with her "I'm trying to work" attitude. As if work was the be-all and end-all. Tension crawled up one side of him and down the other.

"I'm guessing from your description," Mike said, "you two didn't hit things off."

"She threatened to report me to the building association. I told her I was the building association."

"Nice. Now you know why you can't rely on your charm forever."

"We agreed you were going to drop that subject," Grant muttered.

"Merely pointing out that not everyone finds you charming. Though I am surprised you failed with a female."

Grant wasn't so sure he completely failed. "Only because she wasn't my type." Personality-wise, that is. He had no problem with blondes, especially good-looking ones with slender lines and perfect breasts. Unless that is, she was so perfectly put together you could practically feel the hair trying to work free from her ponytail.

Problem was Sophie Messina had felt way too familiar. Dial back a couple years—twenty-eight months to be exact—and he was looking at the female version of his former self.

A sharp knocking sound pulled him from his reverie. Perfect timing. He had a feeling Mike was winding up for another lecture. "My dinner's here."

Soon as he said the words, his stomach began growling. When it came to pizza, he was worse than Pavlov's dog. Giving a silent thank-you to whoever buzzed the deliveryman in, he told Mike he'd call him later in the week.

The pizza man was impatient. He knocked again. Grabbing his wallet, he strode to the front door, mouth already watering.

Except, he discovered upon opening the door, it wasn't the pizza man. Instead, he found a very hot and bothered Sophie Messina, her arms folded across the very chest he'd just been thinking about.

"You took my water," she charged, eyes flashing. "And I want it back."

It took Grant a full minute to comprehend what Sophie was saying, partially because he barely recognized her. In fact, if pressed, he'd be hard to say this was the same person. The woman he met over the weekend had been glossy and tightly wound.

This woman though... Everything about her looked soft, right down to the way the front of her ponytail hung in long lazy curls around her face. One particularly twirly strand drooped over her left eye and practically begged to be brushed aside. And her lips.... He couldn't believe he didn't notice those succulent bee-stung lips on Saturday. The very male parts of his body stirred with appreciation. What had he been thinking about her not being his type?

"Well?" she asked, tapping her foot. "Are you going to turn it back on?"

"Turn what on?" he asked, distracted by the way her eyes switched hues. From deep blue to turquoise and back. He hadn't noticed those before, either.

"There's no need to stare at me like I have three heads," she said. "There's no running water at my place. You obviously turned the water off when you installed your tub. Since you're finished—" her gaze flickered toward the beer in his hand "—I would like you to turn the water back on so I can shower. As you can see, I'm badly in need of one."

Not from where he stood. But, that was neither here nor there. "Impossible," he said, getting back to her accusation.

Her eyes narrowed. Her smudged mascara gave them a sultry, smoky look that managed to transcend her scowl. "Why not?"

"I didn't turn it off."

"Then who did?"

"Beats me," he replied. "Did you pay your water bill?"

She stiffened, pulling her ramrod spine a little tighter. "I always pay my bills."

"Whoa, take it easy," he said, holding up his hands. *Damn.* He figured she'd be unamused, but the way she spat the words you'd think he'd delivered a blow. "I'm sure you do. I was just making a joke."

"I'm afraid I don't have much of a sense of humor right now."

No kidding. He would have said as much, but at that moment her shoulders sagged a little. "It's been a really long day and I just want to take a shower."

She said it with such longing, so much like a little girl who missed out on getting a treat, Grant couldn't help but actually feel a little for her. Enough to give her a straight answer anyway. "Wish I could help you, but the only water I had anything to do with in this building is my own, and I turned that back on yesterday."

"Any chance you turned mine off by mistake?"

"If I did, how would you have taken a shower this morning?

His question cut off that argument. "Besides, even if I did turn my water off today—which I didn't—every unit has its own meter. You have to turn off each one individually."

"Are you sure?"

She didn't give up easily did she? "Positive.

You're either going to have to wait for a plumber or shower somewhere else."

"Terrific." Her shoulders sagged a little more, and Grant swore for a moment when he saw dampness well up in her eyes. "Guess I better start making some phone calls." She turned and headed down the hall only to stop halfway, as if remembering something. "Wait a moment. Isn't this your job?"

"Excuse me?"

"You said you were head of the building association. Isn't it your job to look into building problems?"

Oh, that was rich. First she spends a month slipping notes under his door, then she accuses him of water theft, and now she wanted him to fix her plumbing? "Only regarding common areas," he clarified.

"Plumbing's common."

"Nice try." But like her complaint to the so-called building association, it wasn't going to work. "You're on your own, sweetheart."

"What else is new?" At least that's what it sounded like she muttered. She resumed her retreat, although this time her walk looked suspiciously like trudging.

Damn. Did she have to look so defeated? As if she were about to break? Guilt began snaking its way into his stomach. No way could he ignore that kind of distress. "Hold on," he called out. "I suppose I could look in the basement. Maybe give you an idea of what to tell the plumber."

"Thank you. If you don't mind, I would appreciate it."

He minded, Grant said to himself. He just couldn't say no.

Sophie continued her way downstairs, trying to decide if she felt foolish or justified. On one hand, seeing as how Mr. Templeton had disturbed her past four weekends, checking out her pipes was the least the man could do. On the other, barging upstairs and accusing him of water theft bordered on crazy lady behavior. For someone who believed in being aloof and in control she wasn't doing a very good job. Templeton started it though, by shutting the door in her face and acting all flirty. She'd been stirred up for the past two days, and now, between the sweat and the work and the bumpy subway guy, she wasn't thinking rationally. That was her excuse.

It was also, no doubt, why his presence felt as though it was looming behind her. The back of her nylon running shorts insisted on sticking to her thighs, so that when she stepped down, the material would pull upward, and, Sophie was certain, reveal way too much bare skin. Even though a man her neighbor's age probably wouldn't notice or care about her legs, she felt exposed. Which was interesting because she'd just ridden on two subway cars in the same outfit without a second thought. Then again, no one on the subway looked like her neighbor, either.

Two steps from the bottom she made a decision. They would have to pass her door on the way to the basement. She could slip into her apartment and ditch the shorts in favor of something more appropriate. That way, when he reported back about the pipes, she'd be rid of this weird self-consciousness.

Unfortunately, her front door was where her neighbor chose to catch up. "Oh, no you don't," he said when he saw her reach for the door handle. He caught her elbow with his hand. "You're coming with me."

Her pulse picked up. This new position had him standing almost as close as her subway friend. Either that or her awareness of him had increased again because he sure *felt* close. "I beg your pardon?"

"You're coming downstairs with me so we can both learn what the problem is together."

"But I don't know anything about plumbing."

"Doesn't matter. I want you to see that I checked everything out thoroughly."

She supposed she deserved that. "Fine." Stepping sideways, she broke contact, silently advising him to take the lead. If she was going downstairs to the basement with him, she could at least avoid the skin on the back of her neck prickling.

Back when it was first built, part of the brownstone's basement had been the servants' kitchen. Thus, instead of being greeted by cold damp air, Sophie found herself stepping into a room that was warm and stifling. She instantly felt the air

close in around her. The lack of adequate lighting didn't help matters, either. There were, she
knew, a line of overhead lights, but her guide
apparently didn't need to use them. Instead, he
deftly navigated the space using the dim glow
of the night-light. Sophie followed along. They
walked past the storage cages and the skeleton of
the building's dumbwaiter and through the opening that led to the rear portion of the room. Here
the air was slightly cooler but not by much. Lack
of windows or space erased any air circulation
that might have existed.

A cobweb dangling from the ceiling beam tickled Sophie's face. She wiped it away, spitting
imaginary strands from her lips.

Oblivious, her neighbor pointed toward the rear
of the room where the heating units sat side by
side. Perpendicular to them was a series of pipes
with levers, each connected to a pipe feeding upward. He stopped in front of the first one on the
left and bent down to study the joint.

"I think I found your culprit," he announced.
"Come here."

She tiptoed forward.

"This set of pipes feeds to your apartment. Though I can't tell for sure, I'd guess your gate valve is broken."

"My what?" Peering over his broad shoulder, all Sophie saw was a collection of copper tubing.

"When they laid the pipes, the plumbers must have used an old kind of valve. Sometimes, when debris breaks off from inside the pipe, it knocks down the gate inside, blocking the water flow. I'm betting that's what happened here. The water came in through the main pipe, and then got blocked at the base of your pipe." He turned and gave a smirk from over his shoulder. "You can feel free to apologize at any time."

Apparently, the blood flow to her cheeks wasn't blocked because her face flushed with chagrin. "Can you fix it?" she asked. He was a contractor, right? She'd gladly pay him to get her shower running.

True to the rest of her day, however, he answered with a shake of his head. "Not without ticking off most of the area's plumbers. Repairs like this are out of my jurisdiction, so to speak. You're going to have to call a professional."

And so, she was back to square one. Her skin began to prickle, a sure sign stress was raising her adrenaline. Just what she needed; more sweat. Where was she going to find a plumber that made late-night house calls? More likely she was going to have to waste a chunk of her day tomorrow waiting on one. Leaving her more behind than ever, because Lord knows Allen wouldn't care what she had to stay home for. *That's why we gave you a laptop and smart phone, Sophie.* She let out a decidedly unladylike oath.

"You're welcome," a deep voice replied.

Once again put in her place, Sophie cringed. "I'm sorry," she said, brushing hair and cobwebs from her eyes. "I don't mean to take my frustration out on you."

"You sure? Why stop now?"

The remark made her smile, albeit ruefully. "I have been acting difficult, haven't I? Sorry about that, too."

He shrugged. "As long as we're apologizing, I might have played a small part in your bad attitude."

"When you say 'small,' are you talking about the banging or slamming the door in my face?"

"I did not slam the door. I shut it." In the dim light, Sophie caught the gleam of bright white teeth. "The high ceilings made the noise sound louder."

"My mistake then."

"Apology accepted."

Sophie brushed the hair from her eyes again—stupid curls refused to stay in place—grateful the darkened atmosphere shrouded her appearance. With their business in the basement now finished, she should be heading back upstairs to start looking for a plumber. Her feet didn't feel like moving, though. Instead, she leaned against the chain-link cage behind her, hooking her fingers through the gaps in the pattern. "I think we both got off on the wrong foot," she heard herself say. "I'm not normally such a witch."

"Sure you want to use a *W?*"

"Very funny. And, I'm normally not that, either. Although my assistants might disagree."

"I see. You're one of *those* bosses."

She drew her brow. "Those bosses?"

"The kind that demand a lot from their employees."

"If you mean I have high expectations, then yes, I am."

She could almost imagine him analyzing her words, and out of habit jutted her chin at him in silent challenge. Work hard and work smart. What was wrong with that?

"There's only one problem with that statement." He strolled toward her, his figure casting a towering shadow on the wall. "I don't work for you."

"I know that," she replied.

"You sure?" He smiled again, his curvy grin curving crookedly across his face. "Because the last couple of days you seemed to have a different impression."

Sophie's cheeks flushed again. Good Lord, but she'd blushed more in the past couple of minutes than in the past year. This man definitely made her act out of character. "Is that your way of asking for another apology?"

"Just making sure you don't forget the true nature of our relationship."

"Which is?"

"At the moment, barely civil neighbors, although I suppose now that we've buried the hatchet, we could drop the *barely*."

He strode a little closer, until the space between them wasn't more than a few feet. Without thinking, her eyes dropped to the V of his shirt and the patch of smooth skin peering out of the gap. His skin smelled faintly of beer and peppermint. Its aroma lingered in the basement air like a masculine perfume. Wonder if his skin tasted as good as it smelled.

What on earth…? Since when did she think such kinds of things, about relative strangers no less. For goodness' sake, she didn't even know the man's full…

"Name!"

In the quiet basement, the word came out louder than necessary, causing them both to jump. "I mean, I don't know your name," she quickly corrected. "Only your first initial. From the mailbox."

"Grant."

"Grant," she repeated. That was better. Knowing his name made it better. That is, made him less of a stranger. She still had no business thinking about his skin. Extending her hand, she pushed all inappropriate thoughts out of her head. "What do you say we start fresh? I'm Sophie Messina."

"Nice to meet you, Sophie Messina."

His handshake was firm and strong, not the soft grip so many men adapted when greeting a woman. Sophie could feel the calluses pressing rough against her palm. They were hardworking hands. The sensation conjured up images of work-hewn muscles rippling under exertion.

Lifting her eyes, she caught the spark of… something…as it passed across his caramel-colored eyes, bright enough to light them up despite the shadows, and briefly she insisted their gaze dropped to her lips. Sophie's mouth ran dry at the thought. He cleared his throat, alerting her to the fact she still held his hand. Quickly she released his grip, and they stood there, awkwardly looking at one another.

Somewhere in the distance, a bell rang.

No, not a bell. A buzzer. Once. Twice. Then nothing.

"Dammit, I forgot…"

She stumbled slightly as Grant rushed past her. "Forgot what? What's wrong?"

He didn't answer. He was too busy taking the steps two at a time.

"Wait!" she heard him call to someone from the top of the stairs. It took her a second to catch up, but when she did, she found him standing in the foyer, front door open, staring at the traffic passing in the street. A missed date?

He glared at her from over his shoulder. "You owe me a dinner."

For the second time that evening, Sophie heard herself saying, "I beg your pardon?"

"That," he said, nodding toward the front door, "was my dinner. I missed the delivery because I was downstairs showing you the broken meter."

In other unspoken words, he blamed her.

"I'm sure if you call, he'll turn right around."

Another glare, this one accompanied by him jamming his fingers through his hair and mussing it. If only disheveled looked that good on her. "It was pizza from Chezzerones."

"Oh." Sophie was beginning to understand. Chezzerones had the best pizza in the area, as well as a very strict delivery policy. Fail to answer the door and your number got put on the "bad" list. Something to do with drunken university students and too many wasted calls. Sophie made the mistake of inquiring and had gotten a very detailed explanation from Chezzerone himself one night. It looked like, by helping her, Grant had gotten himself stuck on the bad list.

Darn it all, she *did* owe him a dinner.

CHAPTER THREE

LAST thing Sophie wanted was to have a debt hanging over her head. "All right, come with me," she said.

This time Grant was the one who scowled. "Why?"

"For dinner. You said I owed you a dinner. I'm paying you back. Now come with me."

As she fished her keys from her pocket to unlock her door, she once again felt him standing close, his peppermint scent finding a way to tease her from behind. A flash of heat found its way to the base of her spine.

What was with her? Lord, you'd think she'd had never crossed paths with a good-looking man before.

She so needed a shower and good night's sleep.

Of all the co-op residences in the building, Sophie's was the largest. U-shaped, the apartment reached around the back stairway onto the other side, where the master bedroom was located. The main living area was really two rooms, a parlor turned living room and a dining area. Both rooms featured the same heavy black woodwork as the foyer and contained beautifully scrolled wood and marble fireplaces. The kitchen was located in the rear, on the other side of the dining room. Having let them in, Sophie headed in that direction only to find Grant hadn't followed. Turning, she found him studying the framework dividing the two spaces.

"You kept the doors," he noted, tracing a finger along the molding.

He meant the pocket doors, which could be drawn to divide the space. Obviously he'd been in the space before. "For now. I've only been here a month. I figured I should live with the place awhile before making any major changes."

He nodded, and without asking, gave the door a tug. There was a soft scraping sound as the heavy panel moved outward. "Did the Realtor tell you that these are original?" he asked, brushing the dusty wood.

"He mentioned something."

"Etta—Mrs. Feldman, the owner, insisted on keeping a lot of the original fixtures. Most of the other units are far more modernized."

"The Realtor told me that, too." Apologized, really, over the fact that Sophie's hadn't been one of the redesigned spaces.

"My…" She found herself stumbling for a word to describe David. *Companion* was most correct but the word felt awkward on her tongue. Then again, she was finding talking difficult in general watching Grant caress the paneled door with the tenderness of a long-lost lover. "My…friend suggested I remove them and paint all the woodwork white."

"God, I hope not." She swore he winced at the suggestion. Better not to tell him David's full suggestion—that she gut the place. "This is black walnut."

"So?"

"So—" his look was way too condescending for someone so young "—you paint soft wood, like pine. Hard wood like walnut is meant to be shown off."

"I didn't realize wood came with rules."

What she did know was watching him run his hands up and down the woodwork was damn unnerving. The soft brushing sound of calluses against the wood's rough surface made her stomach knot.

"Did you know Mrs. Feldman well?" she asked, pushing the door back into place.

"We met when she turned the building into apartments. She filled me in on the building's history."

"The Realtor told me she was the original owner."

"Well, not the *original* original," he noted. "This building predates the Civil War. But, her husband's family was. The only reason she converted was because she was convinced a developer would gut the place after she died." Sophie swallowed a kernel of guilt on David's behalf. "She fought right to the end to make sure the building retained as much of its original look as possible. Especially her living space. 'You can push me into converting, but you won't make me change my living room,' she used to say."

"Sounds like you two were like-minded."

"Last couple years, I've come round to see her way of thinking." He gave the woodwork one parting swipe.

There was regret in his words that made him sound older than his years. Look older, too, as a melancholy shadow accompanied them, darkening his golden features. Odd.

"I have to confess," she said, trying to break the mood, "I like some of the old fixtures. The entranceway for example. It's nice how the place is both modern and antique at the same time."

"A brilliantly designed blend," he softly replied. Almost sounded as if he was reciting a quote. Again, the words came across as weighted and old.

She had little time to wonder because Grant had crossed the dining room and was already pushing the swinging door leading to her kitchen. After trying to move him along earlier, she now found herself scurrying to catch up. She did only to find he'd stopped short again. This time he was studying the kitchen cabinetry with the same sensual attentiveness. She had to catch herself from bumping square into his back.

"Then there's the kitchen."

Unlike the edge from before, this time she heard a note of amusement in his voice. Though she couldn't see his face—she was still stuck behind his broad back—Sophie could easily picture his expression, basing the image on the many amused looks he'd shot in her direction over the past two days. Interestingly, in hindsight, those looks weren't nearly as infuriating as they seemed at the time.

"You don't like this room?" she asked.

"Etta was stubborn. She insisted on keeping it as is. Right down to the hardware. Making a last stand, I suppose."

The last line was said as he knelt down to examine a lower cabinet door. Sophie took advantage of the movement to slip past, sucking in her breath to avoid brushing up against him. Her neighbor, attention on the cabinet, didn't appear to notice.

"Maybe she simply knew her mind."

"That she did. Your hinges need replacing," he added, opening the cabinet door.

"I wouldn't mind replacing the entire room." Although she spent little time in the kitchen, Sophie found the space narrow and cramped. She found the room even more cramped now thanks to the addition of Grant's large form. His broad shoulders—so broad they practically filled the expanse between the counters. "Unlike your Mrs. Feldman, I don't need to keep this room exactly as is."

"Won't get an argument from me. Any idea what you'd do?"

Not really. Oh, she had ideas, but they were nebulous and atmospheric, based more on fantasy than any actual plan. "Brighter, definitely," she told him. "Sunnier. With windows and gleaming wood cabinets."

"Sounds like another woman who knows what she wants." Their eyes met, and he flashed her a smile that implied far more than cabinetry. Or so it felt from the way her insides reacted.

"Pizza," she announced abruptly. Goodness but the kitchen was cramped. And really warm.

There was absolutely no air circulation at all on these hot nights. "What kind would you like?"

"I have a choice?"

"Of course. I might not match Chezzerones, but I have a decent variety. Cheese, pepperoni, Hawaiian, chicken, pepper and onion…"

"Holy cow!" His voice sounded from over her shoulder causing her to jump. The guy didn't believe in personal space, did he? "It's like looking at the frozen food section at the mini-mart."

"I like to keep food on hand in case of an emergency is all."

"What kind of emergency? Armageddon?"

Ignoring the comment, Sophie reached into the freezer. Gooseflesh had begun crawling in the wake of his breath on her bare neck, putting her out of sorts again. She'd feel better once she was alone again.

"Here," she said, pulling a box from the stack and thrusting it into his hands. "Go Hawaiian."

He looked down at the box, then back up at her.

"Is there a problem?" she asked him.

"What about cooking?"

She pointed to the side of the box. "Directions

are right here. I don't have my reading glasses, but I'm pretty sure you preheat the oven to four-twenty-five."

"Okay." He didn't budge. Clearly he expected her to cook for him.

Sophie let out a frustrated sigh. It had been way too long a day, and she still had to track down a plumber and finish her paperwork. She didn't have time to entertain her neighbor. Especially one that had her set off balance since their first meeting.

She opened her mouth to tell him exactly that when a sound interrupted the kitchen's silence.

It was her stomach growling.

"Fine," she said, snatching the box back. "I'll cook. But you're on your own for dinner company."

With the pizza safely in the oven, Sophie excused herself and escaped to her bedroom. Hopefully, by freshening up, she could regain the self-control that seemed to be eluding her these past couple days and become more herself. Arguing about pizza? Thinking about what his skin tasted like? Not exactly the most mature of behaviors.

Don't forget barging up to his apartment like a madwoman.

She meant what she told him in the kitchen. He better not expect company. She had way too much to do.

Case in point. Her smart phone told her she'd missed eleven messages since arriving home. Make that a dozen, she amended as her in-box buzzed again.

There was a box of moist wipes in the bottom drawer of her vanity. She grabbed a handful to give herself a makeshift sponge bath. Not as refreshing as a shower, but she felt a little cleaner. "Score one for being prepared," she said as she used one to dampen down her hair. She combed out her ponytail and exchanged her running clothes for a jersey-knit maxi dress.

In the middle of touching up her eyeliner, she paused. *What are you doing, Sophie? Freshening up or fixing up?* She stared at her reflection. Instantly her eyes went to the deepening lines around her eyes and mouth. Two decades of adulthood lay behind those lines. And yet here she was so frazzled by a…a…a boy she was putting on eyeliner to eat frozen pizza.

"Get a grip," she snapped at herself. For goodness' sake, she wasn't some cougar on the prowl. There was absolutely no reason to let her neighbor get to her like this. Setting down the eyeliner, she grabbed a brush instead and combed her hair into a sleek damp bun. Much better, she decided. She looked more like herself again.

During her absence, Grant had moved into the dining room. Soon as she walked in, he looked up, and she swore the corners of his mouth turned downward. "What?" she asked smoothing the sides of her hair.

"You changed."

Why did he sound as if he meant more than clothes? Really, she chided, she had to stop reading undercurrents in everything. Whatever tone Grant had, real or imagined, was irrelevant. The guy was here because she owed him dinner. Soon as he ate, he would leave and most likely, their paths wouldn't cross again.

The rattle of plates pulled her from her thoughts.

Suddenly she realized Grant wasn't merely in the dining room, he was moving around the dining room table.

"What are you doing?" she asked him.

"Isn't it obvious? I'm setting the table."

"So I see." He must have gone through her kitchen because there were plates and flatware on the table. The only thing missing were her linen napkins. Two folded paper towels took their place. "But why?"

"Food's got to go on something." He disappeared back into the kitchen. Sophie followed and found him looking in the fridge. "Only a half-dozen choices. What happened? You get tired by the time you reached the beverage department?"

"Sorry to disappoint you," she replied. She was caught between annoyance and her desire to stare at how his shirt pulled up when he was bent over, exposing the smooth skin beneath. It was the skin that was keeping her from being overly annoyed at his prowling in her kitchen.

"Relax, I was joking. It's actually a damn impressive selection. You even have my favorite brand of beer." He waved an amber-colored bottle. "Would you like one? Or are you more of a wine woman?"

"Actually I don't drink."

"At all?"

Sophie shook her head. "My mother had a drinking problem."

"I'm sorry."

"Don't be. She wasn't your mother." Usually she simply told people alcohol didn't appeal to her and left it at that, but for some reason tonight the response had felt too trite. Seeing the awkwardness passing across Grant's face, however, reminded her why she preferred not to share the truth. "Anyway, now I only keep liquor on hand for entertaining." Which, she reminded herself, she was decidedly *not* doing.

According to the timer, the pizza was almost ready so she grabbed an oven mitt from a nearby hook. "Don't forget," she said, as she removed the baking sheet, "you're on your own for dinner. I don't care if you use my table and plates, but don't expect conversation. I have work to do."

"You work an awful lot."

"Comes with the territory. Stock market never rests, so neither do I."

"Never? You don't even take time out to go to bed?"

Sophie's hand slipped, sending the cutter careening up and over the edge of the crust. From the corner of her eye, she caught Grant trying to hide his smirk.

"I manage to grab a few hours' sleep," she answered. Pretending she didn't catch the innuendo, even though they both knew otherwise. "Some nights more than others. Some nights, like last night and tonight, less. Depends on how many interruptions I have." He wasn't the only one who could shoot off a veiled comment.

Unfortunately, unlike her, he didn't suffer an embarrassing reaction. Instead, he played with the edge of his beer label. "Do you ever wonder if it's worth the effort?"

"Of course it is. How else is a person going to move up?" she asked just before pushing the swinging door. "The world doesn't hand you success. You want something, you have to go for it."

She set the pizza in the center of the table, then

took a seat in her usual chair. Grant settled in the spot across from her. Even with a table in between, the setup managed to feel cozy and Sophie wondered if letting him stay was a good idea. How long had it been since she'd shared a dinner at home with someone? Never as far as this place was concerned. David preferred eating out and before him… Wow, she couldn't remember the last time.

A few inches from her right hand, her BlackBerry blinked, telling her she had another email. The total from Allen was already up to fifteen. Meanwhile, across the table, Grant was smacking his lips in overly dramatic fashion. "Not bad," she heard him say. "Not Chezzerones quality, but for a frozen pizza, it's pretty good."

"Glad to know my mini-mart meets your high standards." She was busy typing an email to Allen before her in-box buzzed again.

"You should try a slice."

"I will."

"I mean before the pizza gets cold."

She looked up and he immediately held up a hand. "I know. You're working. Doesn't end, does it? The pressure. No matter how much you accomplish, there's always something more to be done."

"Clearly you've seen my to-do list."

There was a pause while he took another bite. "Do you mind if I ask a personal question?"

Sophie felt her heart skitter. "Personal how?" she asked, looking up.

"What goal are you trying to reach with all this work?"

Oh. That wasn't what she expected. "I told you in the kitchen. I want to get ahead."

"Just ahead."

With a sigh, she put aside her phone. Obviously her "guest" had no intention of letting her email until she answered him. "My plan is to be named managing director of my firm."

"Ambitious. Then what?"

"Then I'll be at the top of the food chain." She'll have climbed higher than anyone expected a member of the Messina family to climb—including members of the Messina family. "And then I'll be the one pestering people with emails."

"Sounds like you've got everything planned out."

"I do." Although she didn't owe him any further explanation, she decided to give him one anyway. Who knows, maybe he'd learn something from the advice. *Like you're interested in mentoring him.* "I came in as a junior investment analyst, worked my way up to senior and with time and effort, I'll move up to the next level. In fact, rumor has it one of our directors is retiring, putting me in a very good position to take his place."

"Then what?"

It was like answering a broken record. Then what. Then what. "Then I can focus on the other items on my list."

"Items?" Reaching over, he lay a slice of pizza on her plate. "Here. Eat or be eaten. What do you mean by 'items on your list'?"

Sophie sighed again. "I didn't realize dinner came with an inquisition."

"I'm curious."

"All right. If you must know, I have a Life To-do List. Goals I want to accomplish." Everything she

needed to officially consider herself having succeeded in life. A college degree. An MBA. A
house of her own. A high-powered job. A successful, mature companion. A summerhouse.

"Like a bucket list."

"More like a master life plan."

Grant was nodding as he raised his drink.
"How very…rigid of you," he said.

Rigid? Maybe but rigidity had served her well
so far. More than he'd ever know. That sexy smile
probably never encountered a hurdle in its life.
"Don't you believe in planning for the future?"

To her surprise, the question caused his jaw
muscles to tense. His eyes grew distant and dark.
Only for a second, though, then the darkness disappeared, replaced by a lopsided grin. "Where's
the surprise in that?"

"I'm not big into surprises. I prefer forewarn-
ing and foundation. When you're older, you'll
understand."

The lopsided grin slid into sexy territory. "Are
you trying to sound like my mother on purpose?"

"Why not? I'm almost old enough to be."

"Hardly."

"All right, maybe not that old. But I am old enough. Older than you." And apparently felt the need to remind both of them of that fact.

He took a drink. "I wouldn't go filling out your nursing home application quite yet. And trust me, you look nothing like my mother." As if to prove his point, he let his gaze travel from the top of her head to her waist.

Feeling her self-consciousness threatening to rise again, she used her pizza as an excuse to look away. Didn't matter. As she tore her crust into tiny bites, she could still feel the warmth flooding her cheeks. Scrutiny, even flattering scrutiny, was never something she enjoyed. Reminded her too much of unwanted attention. Over the years she'd cultivated a tolerance for being looked at, but for some reason her neighbor's gaze penetrated deeper than most. Its imprint lingered on her nervous system, feeding her awareness long after the look had ended. It was most disturbing, particularly during moments like this.

The buzz of a cell phone interrupted the silence.

"Duty calls," she heard Grant say.

"Always does." Out of the corner of her eye, she saw the blinking email indicator on her cell phone. Calling to her. She ran her fingers lightly across the face of the phone.

Grant picked up on the hint and pushed away from the table. "Guess I'll be on my way then," he said. "Wouldn't want to derail your trip up the corporate ladder."

"Thank you," she replied. There seemed an underscoring of sarcasm in that comment, but she chose to ignore it.

"Thank you for the pizza."

"Does this mean we're even now?"

"Even?"

"For costing you dinner. And accusing you of stealing my water," she added.

In Sophie's mind, the appropriate answer would have been "don't worry about it." At least that's the response she would give. Instead, he gave her another one of those long unnerving looks. One that wrapped itself tightly around her and squeezed. "We'll see."

We'll see? What kind of answer was that? Either they were even or they weren't. *We'll see* implied unfinished business. She hated unfinished business. Absolutely loathed it. Why on earth would he imply something like that?

And why did her insides do a little tumble at the prospect?

Grant let himself out. Sophie was already on her phone and didn't notice. Click, click, clicking her way on her climb to what was it? Managing director? Listening to her talk about her "master plan" made his blood chill. It all sounded so determined, so calculated. And oh so achingly familiar.

The night had started out so differently. Order pizza, kick back and watch the game. A simple enough plan. Who decided to add Reminders of Mistakes Past to the agenda? First Mike, then his sexy workaholic neighbor.

Heaving a sigh, he washed a hand across his features and headed toward the staircase. Seeing Etta's apartment in all its untouched splendor didn't help. Bad enough he got a stab of guilt every time he mounted the staircase.

He wrapped his hand around the banister. Days

of use had already worn the gloss away, creating a dull but warm-looking patina. The way wood should be, he thought, stroking the grain. God, but this house had been magnificent in its original form. Time worn, but with all the previous grandeur still alive beneath the surface.

And you helped talk her into chopping up the place. Yet another example of how blind he'd been to the obvious back then.

At least he was doing his best to repair the damage now. His apartment was one of the few mistakes he could fix.

For some reason, his thoughts drifted back to the first floor apartment and the woman working away at her dining room table. Bet if he knocked on her door three hours from now, she'd still be sitting in the same place, BlackBerry in hand, pizza untouched. A complete waste of legs and beauty if you asked him.

She reminded him of someone. Other than himself, that is. He'd been racking his brain all evening trying to figure out who, and he couldn't. Definitely not his mother, that's for sure. Last time he checked, his mother didn't have lips as ripe as berries. Too bad Sophie was such a work-aholic, or he'd have tried a little harder to taste them.

On the other hand, maybe he should try to taste them *because* she was a workaholic. Show her what she was missing. After all the woman could use some loosening up. If anyone knew the cost of tunnel vision it was him. Besides, he'd never met a blonde he didn't want to kiss, and those lips were far too delicious looking to pass up.

Yup, he thought as he reached his apartment door, he was definitely going to have to give this idea some thought.

CHAPTER FOUR

NEXT morning Sophie woke to the sound of someone knocking on her door. And she'd been right in the middle of a good dream, too. At least she assumed it was good. Only the sensation remained. Prying open one eye, she saw the time and groaned. After last night's impromptu dinner, she'd stayed up late catching up on the market activity she missed. Her reward to herself was to be sleeping in to six-thirty. That's when David would be picking her up so she could shower at his place. He'd originally suggested she come over last night, but she'd begged off, insisting she needed to work. In reality, she was reluctant to start a pattern.

Not to mention you felt a little awkward after spending part of the night flirting with your man-child neighbor.

The knocking started anew. She slipped on her

robe, ran a comb through her hair—thank heaven for ponytails, bed head's best friend—and padded into the living room just in time to call off round three. "Coming!"

"Good morning," Grant greeted when she opened the door. He looked entirely too fresh and showered for so early in the morning. His bright blue shirt clung to his shoulders almost as obscenely as his jeans clung to his hips. The attraction she fought all last night came rolling back so strongly her knees almost buckled. "Do you have any idea what time it is?" she asked him, tightening the belt on her robe.

His expression was unapologetic. "Is that any way to greet the men who fixed your water?"

"You fixed my water?"

"Not me, him." Belatedly, Sophie realized Grant wasn't alone. An African-American man with salt-and-pepper hair stood next to him. He carried a toolbox and wore a blue-and-white-striped work shirt with a patch that read A Plus Plumbing.

"This—" Grant clapped the man on his shoulder "—this is Erik Alvareen. Only plumber you'll ever need."

Sophie was still a little fuzzy. Grant had called a plumber? For her? Why? She shook the man's hand. "Sorry for the abrupt greeting. I had no idea you would be by."

"Normally, I wouldn't show up this early," Erik explained, "but I've got another job midtown that's gonna take most of the day."

"Plus, he owes me," Grant added, giving the man's shoulder a squeeze.

"Not anymore I don't," Erik replied. "You dragging my rear end out of bed at four in the morning makes us even."

"Like you weren't going to be awake anyhow. Erik's already looked at the meter," Grant told Sophie, "but he wanted to check your faucets, too."

"Just to make sure. Best to cover all bases."

As if she could argue with that. Sophie stepped aside and let the two men in.

"Do you mind if I take a second to throw some clothes on?" she asked, tugging on her belt again. For the second day in a row, Grant managed to find her in her skimpy clothing. This morning's short robe was perfect for hot weather, but not for entertaining two men. Especially Grant, whose eyes immediately dropped to the hemline.

"Don't bother on our account," he said.

The remark did not help. Sophie could feel her skin turning red. What was he doing here, anyway? The plumber seemed to have everything well in hand.

"I'll only be a minute," she told them. "If you'd like, you can check out the kitchen first. Grant knows where it is."

When she returned five minutes later in a far more appropriate set of yoga pants and T-shirt, she found Grant alone. "Erik is looking at the guest bathroom," he said.

Much to her irritation, Grant had found both her collection of coffee and her coffee mugs and was operating her single-cup coffeemaker. "I don't recall offering you free rein to dig through my cupboards."

"I didn't dig anywhere. I saw the coffee last night when I was getting the plates." The mug finished brewing and he handed it to her. "Figured you might be looking for some caffeine since we dragged you out of bed so early."

All right, she'd forgive him the intrusion this time. "The plumber was a surprise," she said, scooting by him to get to the refrigerator. "You didn't have to do that."

"I didn't want to risk a complaint being filed with the building association. Besides, Erik is the one guy I know who will do the repair right."

"I have to admit, I do appreciate things being done right," Sophie conceded.

He popped another pod into the brewing chamber. "Why am I not surprised?"

Finished doctoring her coffee, Sophie offered him the nonfat creamer only to have him shake his head. "No thanks. I'm more a black and bold kind of guy."

"Bold, anyway," she murmured, thinking how he made himself at home. And at home was exactly how he looked, too. Propped against the countertop, his long legs crossed at the ankles, he looked custom built for the space. The hem of his T-shirt ghosted the top of his low-slung jeans, just short enough so that when he moved his arms it inched upward revealing a sliver of plaid, from his boxers. Sophie cursed the warmth that unfurled in her stomach. It was way too early in the morning for such overt virility.

She gripped her mug a little tighter and positioned herself across the aisle. "Are you always like this?" she asked him.

"Bold? Absolutely."

Ignoring the way his answer seemed to slide down her spine, she said, "I mean, do you always do favors for strangers? Especially ones who have been—"

"A pain in the butt?"

"I was going to say 'at odds.'"

"Tomato, tomahto. I thought we settled all that with last night's pizza."

Had they? She seemed to recall a sense of unfinished business. "Either way, it was still nice of you. I'm looking forward to taking a shower."

"Glad I could help. Although, if you ask me," he said with a slow smile, "you also look pretty damn good for a woman who's been denied bathing privileges."

"Benefits of bottled water."

"Very resourceful. Somewhere there's a Boy Scout leader wishing you were in his troop. You'd be the queen of merit badges."

"Thank you."

"What makes you certain I'm giving you a compliment?"

"I'll take it as one." Cradling her mug, she fortified herself with a good long sip. She could already feel the caffeine in her bloodstream, kicking up her pulse and causing her insides to churn. At least she chose to blame the caffeine. She refused to acknowledge the voice in the back of her head suggesting her company was having the greater effect. "Same way I'll attribute your mocking to jealousy."

"Jealousy?"

"Sure. Because I'd earn more merit badges than you."

He laughed. "I'll have you know that no one earned more merit badges than I did back in Scouts. I mastered every skill. I can even rub two sticks together and make fire."

His feral smile was making Sophie's knees

buckle. If she hadn't been holding her coffee, she'd have gripped the countertop.

Heat pooled at the base of her spine. At some point during their exchange, she'd leaned forward, bringing her into his physical space. Peppermint reached her nostrils. She was close enough now to see the faint lines near the corners of his eyes.

And, he was close enough to see the bags under hers.

She practically slammed her spine against the counter edge straightening her back. "So," she said, covering by taking another healthy gulp of coffee. "Four o'clock in the morning, huh? Your friend Erik must have owed you one heck of a favor. What did you do?"

"Nothing big. I helped his grandson out of a jam this past winter is all."

"More like he bailed the boy's sorry ass out of jail," Erik said, bursting through the swinging door. "You're all set," he said to Sophie. "I checked all the faucets, and they're working fine."

She suppressed the urge to hug him. "You have no idea how happy I am to hear you say so. You forget how much you depend on running water until you don't have it for a few hours. Thank you so much."

"Anything for a 'friend' of Grant's," the older man replied with a knowing grin. Sophie was so grateful for his assistance, she let the misunderstanding slide. "Besides, my wife would have killed me if she ever caught me making a lady wait for her shower."

"You're wife's a wise woman," she told him.

After having her coffee offer declined and promising she would call him for all her plumbing needs, Sophie walked Erik to the door. She assumed Grant would leave with his friend as well, but he surprised her, hanging back in her doorway.

"Still have half a cup of coffee," he pointed out when she shot him a frown.

Sophie tried to work up some indignation but couldn't. He did, after all, get her water back. "You really didn't have to make the man come by so early," she said, pushing open the kitchen door.

"You'd rather wait all day?"

"Absolutely not. I love the fact he stopped here

first." It saved her from having to trek all her belongings to David's apartment, along with keeping her from wasting part of her morning on the phone.

She contemplated the liquid in her cup, thinking once again how the color resembled Grant's eyes. There was a question she'd wanted to ask since Erik spoke earlier. "Was he telling the truth? Did you bail his grandson out of jail?"

He waved off the incident as though he was chasing off a fly. "Kid was in the wrong place at the wrong time is all. Erik and I were working on a project together at the time, so when Bryant couldn't reach his grandfather, he called me."

And Grant rode to his rescue? She thought of other late-night phone calls. The shrill ringing of the phone shattering whatever temporary calm had settled in the apartment. The pleas for help. The promises that this time would be the last time. Didn't matter which parent made the promise because there never was a last time. There was only chaos and drama. So much drama it made you sick. Until you moved as far away as possible and hoped those phone calls would never find you again.

"He's lucky you took the call," she said quietly.

A dark look came over his bright features, so dark it made her forget her own shadows. "That time, anyway," he said over the rim of his coffee cup.

"Bryant gets into trouble often?"

"What?" He looked surprised she'd spoken. "No," he said, quickly shaking his head. "Not at all. That was a one-time, stupid kid mistake. He learned his lesson."

What then caused the shadow that crossed his face? The bleak, distant state that killed the sparkle in his eyes. Grant Templeton wasn't as laid-back and carefree as he would like the world to believe.

Conversation over, they stood and sipped their coffee in quiet. A strange kind of silence, it was, too. Unnerving and serene at the same time. For while she was far too aware of his presence—the way he breathed through his nose, the rustle of fabric when he raised his arm, the soft slurp when he sipped his coffee—she found the sounds strangely natural. They were the kinds of sounds she always imagined a home would be full of.

In the back of her mind she knew she should get to her much anticipated shower, but she didn't move. It was the need for more caffeine. Two nights with too little sleep had her needing extra fortification.

Keep telling yourself that, Sophie.

"Behind you." Grant's voice broke the silence. "That's where I'd put the window."

Sophie looked over her shoulder and straight into a cabinet door. "You think? What happened to not touching the original fixtures?"

"Guess old habits die harder than I thought." His attention returned to his cup, a little more somber than before. "It really is the perfect spot for a window, though."

Sophie studied the space, trying to picture a window instead of a wood door. She only saw cabinet.

"Would I get sunshine?"

"Enough."

Enough sounded good. "Tell me more." She was starting to get excited. A voice in the back of her head suggested part of her enthusiasm was to brighten his voice again. Even so, she wanted to hear what he had to say.

And boy did she hear. For the next several minutes he laid out suggestions, weaving a spell of mental images that left her captivated. Although to be honest, if asked, she didn't think she could repeat a single idea. What seized her attention was the authority with which he spoke. Clear, strong-voiced. There was no doubting his vision. And the way he demonstrated each idea with his hands—gesturing about the small space with grace and surety—she could easily imagine him making those suggestions reality.

Bet he could do a lot with those hands. She had to bite her lip at the thought.

"Sounds like you've given this a lot of thought," she said when he finished. A lot. Plus he spoke with a knowledge she was ashamed to admit she didn't expect from a young, live-in-the-moment contractor. Another layer to ponder. It was clear he had much more expertise than she gave him credit for.

"More than I should," he admitted. Was that a blush or a shadow on his cheeks?

"Regardless, your ideas are amazing. Too bad I don't know a good contractor."

"Too bad indeed."

The carousel of plastic coffee pods sat on the counter from when Grant first used them. Empty cup in hand, she moved across the room, selected one and popped it into the chamber, all the while trying not to feel Grant's eyes on her. There was a soft gurgling noise and the smell of dark roast coffee filled the air as the machine began brewing.

It was a bad idea. She knew less than nothing about him, even less about his work skills. Regardless, her next words came out before she could stop them. "I don't suppose you're interested."

"Don't sell yourself short, sweetheart."

Oh, but it was way too early in the morning for her stomach to be quivering. "I meant the kitchen. I was wondering if you'd be interested in the job."

"Oh, that."

Could his voice be any flatter? She'd heard him let out a long breath. "We'll see," he answered finally.

Again with the "we'll see." Only this time, instead of being vague, it sounded resigned. "You don't want the job?" Why spend all this time waxing on with ideas then?

"I'm very selective about the jobs I take on," he replied.

"You don't say." She reached to take her mug from the coffeemaker. "I didn't realize contractors could afford to be picky in this economy."

"Historical renovator, and I can," he corrected, joining her on her side of the counter.

The arrogance in his voice was overwhelming, too much so if you asked Sophie. However, if he was trying to hook her interest, the tactic worked. "Tell me then," she asked, unable to help herself, a habit she seemed to have developed around him, "what kind of projects do you take on?"

"Ones that interest me, or that are special. A rare building, an interesting concept."

He was holding something back, but she

couldn't tell what with all the cockiness wrapped around his answer.

"And my kitchen isn't interesting or special?" she had to ask.

"Unfortunately, you're both."

Sophie frowned. "What's that mean?"

"Means you could tempt a man into doing most anything."

Goose bumps ghosted across Sophie's skin. When had he moved so close? And for that matter, were they still talking about her kitchen, because she wasn't so sure.

Callused fingertips caught the edge of her jaw, forcing her face to turn right. His breath smelled of peppermint and coffee. Sophie struggled not to lick her lips.

"Anyone ever tell you that you're incorrigible?" she asked.

He lifted her face closer. Light as his touch was, Sophie could feel every bump and rough patch, every pinprick of pressure against her skin.

"All the time." His eyes dropped to her mouth.

This time Sophie did lick her lips. And held her breath. And leaned closer…

Whoa! Whoa! Whoa! Sophie slammed on the brakes, bringing the moment to a screeching halt by bolting toward the door.

"Will you look at the time?" she babbled, sounding like a complete idiot since, other than the digital display on the microwave behind her, there wasn't a clock in view. "I'm going to be late for work if I don't get into the shower."

"It's only six-thirty."

Figures he could see the clock.

"Exactly. I'm usually on my way to the office by seven." Some days. Never mind she planned on sleeping in today. Inside her stomach, her nerves were doing the triple jump. *Hop, skip, plunge.* What on earth had she been thinking?

She wasn't. That was the problem. Her brain— and body—developed a whole new set of behaviors around him. Ones she didn't recognize.

Like the way her insides shook just now. "I've going to go now," she announced. As if the flight weren't obvious. "Feel free to take your coffee with you. No sense wasting a freshly brewed cup."

"You're the one who brewed the second cup."

"Right. I forgot." Fortunately, she had her back to him so she was spared looking at his amused expression. "Do you mind letting yourself out, as well?"

"If that's what you want me to do."

Okay, he didn't just drop his voice a notch when asking the question, did he? "Yes, that's what I want. Thank you."

Her hand was on the door, and she was about to push when she regained a sliver of her senses. "And thank you again for bringing Erik by. I really appreciate it. Especially after I was so..." Oh, Lord, the word faded right out of her head.

"Anyway, I guess that means I—" inwardly she winced, realized what she was stupidly about to say "—owe you again."

Sophie gasped as his breath tickled the back of her neck. He was standing close again. Whether on purpose or by coincidence, she couldn't say, but from the spreading heat, her body obviously did. "No problem. We can negotiate how you can pay me back another time."

Her arm began to tingle as he leaned even closer, his arm tickling the hair on hers as he

reached past her and laid his hand on the door
next to hers. "Enjoy your shower." Dammit, but
his voice dropped *again.*

"Oh, and by the way," he added, pushing the
door open. "Erik said you might have to let the
hot water run for a bit before it kicks in."

That's all right, thought Sophie, rubbing her
tingling forearm. Cold water would do just fine.

That, Grant thought, watching the door swing
back and forth, was…interesting. Definitely
worth getting up early for. Though he wouldn't
admit it to Erik, he owed the plumber now.

Calling his friend occurred to him last night
during the ninth inning. Right after he pictured
Sophie banging on his door because the plumber
she hired didn't do a good enough job. And while
Sophie on his doorstep wasn't an unpleasant idea,
he figured why not cut short the inevitable glares
by getting the one man he knew would fix the
problem right the first time? Rousting Sophie
from bed had been the added bonus. Gave him
a chance to sneak another peek at the Sophie he

met last night. The clean-scrubbed, mussed-hair Sophie.

Oh, yeah, he definitely owed Erik.

Things did get a little unnerving when he slipped into his old role rattling off design ideas. Scary how easily that happened. Again, it was Sophie. Something about her description last night triggered his inspiration. He found himself wanting to give her the kitchen she envisioned.

In a way, his desire to do so rattled him as much as the slip. Women didn't inspire him for the most part, at least not so far as wanting to please them. Designwise that is. Sophie was the first. His disdain for Etta's kitchen must have gotten to be too much for him to control.

Or it was Sophie. He rubbed his fingers together, reliving the feel of her skin. His neighbor wore flushed well. Real well. Damn shame she backed away before things could get even more interesting.

Next time, he decided. Smiling to himself, he poured Sophie's untouched coffee into his cup. Next time.

* * *

"Everything all right?" David asked when she called. "You sound distracted."

Distracted was an understatement. Try horrified, disturbed, off balance. "Everything's fine." *I almost kissed my upstairs neighbor in the middle of an impromptu job interview is all.* "Late night."

"Figured as much. I caught the early morning financial report. Looks like you'll have an equally busy day."

"I've already heard from Allen." His voice mail had been waiting for her when she retreated from the kitchen. An electronic reminder to keep her head on straight. "We have a meeting first thing."

"Sounds like you've become his regular go-to person in a crisis."

"I think so." You'd get no complaints from her—Allen's favor bode well for when the company decided to name a new manager.

In the distance, she heard the click of her front door; the sound of Grant leaving. After his comment about the water, she'd pushed past him and gone to her bedroom so quickly she hadn't realized he'd lingered. Must have decided to have that coffee after all. Was it her imagination or did the apartment suddenly feel emptier? Had to be her imagination.

"…water back."

"What?" She hadn't realized David spoke.

"I said you must be glad you got your water back."

"Very. You don't know how much you appreciate running water till it's gone." She'd said the same thing to Erik and Grant. "Plus, I don't have to put you out now."

"You weren't putting me out. We could have had coffee."

"True. We'll have to wait till this weekend now." Sophie looked to the floor, a guilty knot in her stomach. Another reason she should be ashamed of her behavior back in the kitchen. She and David had an *understanding*.

"Which reminds me," David said. On the other end of the line, there was the rustle of paper. "This Friday, the Bar's Business Law Division is hosting an event at the Natural History Museum. Networking-wise it makes sense to attend with a guest."

"Sure," she accepted, swallowing her reluctance. After her behavior, she felt too guilty to say no, even if going out on Friday did go against their usual routine.

"Wonderful. The event will be good for you, too. You'll meet some great contacts for when you make managing director."

"Sounds great." Sophie smiled a guilty smile. That was another thing. David understood her priorities. He looked out for her career. He was good for her.

She finished the call by promising to talk with David later in the day. Then, hanging up, she looked at her reflection. The woman in the mirror had a grim expression.

"You should be ashamed of yourself, flirting with Grant like that," Sophie told her. "The man's not even your type for crying out loud."

David was. In fact, he was exactly the kind of man she should be wanting. Stable. Mature. *Age-appropriate*. He wouldn't show up on her doorstep by surprise or turn a discussion about kitchen renovations into some kind of seductive game. Nope. With David, what you saw was what you got. The man he was this Friday night would be the same man she would see next weekend, and all the weekends after that. Consistent. No surprises. No hints of unfinished business. Just the way she preferred.

Simply put, David fitted in to her plans. Her neighbor, with his T-shirts and peppermint aura, did not. End of story.

CHAPTER FIVE

Sophie and Grant didn't cross paths for the rest of the week. Sophie told herself the feeling in her stomach was relief, especially on Thursday when she thought she saw him at the mailbox only to discover it was someone from the fourth floor.

Friday afternoon, however, she came home to find a large white bathtub on the sidewalk. On any normal day, the sight in itself would have startled her, but she was too distracted by the sandy-haired man standing next to the tub.

Hands planted on his narrow hips, Grant didn't notice her approach. Good thing since she needed a moment to recover from the wave of attraction that crashed over her the second she saw him. It was as though the man released pheromones that made her body react as if it had a mind of its own.

Catching her breath, she put on her best nonchalant voice. "Interesting place to install a bathroom."

Caught off guard, Grant looked up quickly, his brown eyes catching the light and looking so close to golden it made Sophie's head swim. "I'm waiting for the delivery guy to park the truck so we can carry her upstairs. Apparently he has a thing about leaving the truck double-parked and unattended."

The tub was large and white with four clawed feet. The kind built for taking a long relaxing soak. Sophie started to picture Grant doing just that then thought better of it. The less she thought of Grant in anything other than a work capacity, the better.

She ran a hand along the smooth white rim. "Shouldn't it be in a box or something?"

"I bought it salvage."

Which, apparently, explained everything. "What now?"

"Soon as Eddie, the driver, gets back, we carry it upstairs. Want to help?"

She shook her head. "No thanks. I'll stick with my nice light briefcase."

"Wimp."

"Maybe so, but at least I won't be complaining about a bad back tomorrow morning."

"But if my back hurts, I'll have this nice big tub to sink into." Leaning over, he knocked on the side, causing a deep clanking noise. "Hear that? Exactly like the kind the original building had."

Though she couldn't care less about antique bathtubs, Sophie nonetheless found herself caught up by the enthusiasm in his voice. The sparkle in his eyes didn't hurt, either. "You certainly take your building history seriously."

"I've learned to." He looked to their building facade. "Do you ever think about how blind we can be to what's right in front of us? We think we're seeing everything, but we miss so much. With old buildings it's like, I don't know, seeing an oyster and not noticing the pearl."

"Unless the oyster didn't have a pearl to begin with," Sophie replied. In her opinion, some pasts were better distanced from, or erased altogether. Take her own past, for example. She doubted there was very much worth polishing there.

"There's always a pearl."

Maybe with buildings, but in the larger scheme, she knew better. Things like lives were best built by looking toward the future. "For someone so young, you are way too romantic."

"For someone not that much older, you aren't nearly enough."

He moved into her space, eyes heavy-lidded as though focused on her mouth. A mouth that had suddenly run dry. Breaking eye contact, she looked instead to the tub. Rubbing her hand along the cool white surface, she said, "I will admit, the tub does look comfortable."

"Want to try her on for size?"

"I beg your pardon?" She laughed. "You want me to get in the tub?"

"Sure, why not?"

"How about the fact it's sitting on the sidewalk?"

"So? Come on, give her a try." Sophie started to protest, but Grant refused to take no for an answer. Instead, he took her hand and the electricity passing up her arm distracted her into silence.

"Go ahead, sit," he urged after he'd led her one leg at a time into the depth. "Stretch out your legs. I want to figure out the maximum height requirements."

"You can't figure it out on your own?"

"I already know I'm too tall. Besides, you owe me a favor, remember?"

Did he have to bring that up? Or say the words in the same maddening murmur? "Couldn't I make you another frozen pizza?"

She hauled one leg over the side. "If my pant-suit gets dirty, you're paying the dry cleaning bill."

"You won't get dirty. Sit."

Sophie sat. The sides of the tub came up to her shoulders and neck. She felt like an idiot. "I mean really sit. Lean back and close your eyes."

She leaned back. She refused to close her eyes however. There were limits.

Grant squatted next to her and rested his chin on the rim. "Can't you picture yourself coming home after a hard day and relaxing in this baby? A candle, some bubble bath, your trusty rubber duck."

The last made her give a rather unladylike

snort. "Somehow I don't picture you as being the wine and bubble bath type."

His eyes grew to a deep dark brown. "I'm into all sorts of things with the right company," he drawled.

Sophie had to press her thighs together to keep her legs from tingling. All of a sudden, her position felt way too intimate in spite of their open surroundings. With Grant behind her, his face hovering next to her ear. The way it might be if they were actually lounging in the bathtub. Why did he have to make everything sound so sexual?

"Can I get out now?" she asked, bolting upright. "The deliverymen are probably on their way back and I'm sure they'd prefer not to have to carry the extra weight." Plus, she'd prefer not to have them arrive while she was stretched out on the sidewalk.

"Sure, but for the record," Grant said, steadying the tub as she scrambled back to her feet, "it wouldn't be that much extra weight."

"Don't you mean, by comparison?" She lifted a leg over the side, wobbling slightly on her heel as she stepped down onto the sidewalk.

Grant caught her by the elbow. "Careful now," he said, "I've got you."

"Thank you."

"Pleasure's all mine."

There he went again; drawling the simplest of words and making her body want to melt. "I wish you wouldn't do that," she said, righting herself.

Grant cocked his head. "Do what?"

"Say things in that voice."

"What voice?"

"You know darn well what voice I mean." He was acting obtuse on purpose. "You sound like you're flirting with me."

Understanding crested across his features along with a slow, sexy smile. "Oh, you mean this voice," he said, automatically dropping to the texture of rough honey.

"Yes, that voice," she snapped. "Please stop."

"Why?"

"Because it's not proper. I'm—"

"A beautiful woman?"

He thought her beautiful?

Stay on point, Sophie. "A prospective customer," she countered. "For that reason alone we should keep things professional."

He looked down into her face. "You make an interesting point."

A point that might hold more weight if she'd thought to break free of his touch. Her elbow was still nestled in his hand; the contact with her skin palpable despite the linen of her blazer.

"I wasn't aware my tone of voice had that much effect."

"It doesn't."

Reluctantly she lifted her arm free. "But given I'm considering hiring you, I figure it's important to be upfront with one another. After all, we've only known each other a couple days. I'd hate for either of us to misunderstand the other's intentions. Or for anyone else to get the wrong impression, for that matter."

"Okay, now you've lost me." He folded his arms. "Why would others get the wrong impression?"

"You know…older woman, younger contractor." He was so not going to make her say it aloud, was he?

"You're afraid people might think you're some cougar taking advantage of a poor innocent boy."

"Hardly." She may not have known Grant Templeton long, but *innocent* was definitely not a word she would use.

"Oh, then you're afraid they'll think I'm taking advantage of the lonely spinster."

"I am not a spinster." And he was pushing her buttons on purpose. She smacked his shoulder. "Be nice to your elders."

"Yes, ma'am," he said, chuckling. "Seriously, though, is it that important to you what people think?"

"Yes." Sophie replied without hesitation. He'd better believe it was important. After how hard she worked to become the woman she was? She wouldn't apologize, either.

Grant sat on the edge of the tub and regarded her. "Why?"

"Long story."

"One of those." He stretched out his legs and crossed them at the ankle. "Maybe one day you'll share it."

Doubtful. Suffice to say not every oyster had a

pearl; some were man-made—or woman-made in this instance. As long as they weren't scrutinized too carefully, no one would know the difference.

"Are you sure your delivery people are coming back?" she asked, changing the subject. The tree-lined street had a number of people, but none looked dressed for moving a bathtub.

"Good question. They better or you won't be the only one who used this tub on the sidewalk. Only I won't be dressed in a linen pantsuit."

That image would be seared into her brain for the night. "Hope you have bail money set," she said, swallowing hard.

Grant grinned. "Worried about answering late-night calls?"

"Depends. If I answer, will I get a price break on my new window?"

Their smiles connected and Sophie found herself getting lost in a dazzle of caramel warmth. Why was it again that she thought maintaining distance was a good idea?

"Sophie?"

David. In a flash the connection fell apart.

Talking with Grant, she completely lost track,

and naturally David was right on time. He wore a pale gray suit and his white shirt was crisp and wrinkle free as usual. His silver hair shined in the early evening sky.

"I thought that was you standing out here." Sophie resisted the urge to duck her head as he leaned in to kiss her cheek. Since when was she shy about David kissing her in public?

Although the public didn't usually involve a pair of caramel eyes watching her.

A frown creased the lines of David's high forehead. "Why is there a bathtub on your sidewalk?"

"Grant's waiting for the deliverymen to park their truck."

"And Sophie was graciously warning me about the dangers of bathing in public," Grant added, causing Sophie to blush again.

"A wise warning," David replied. He stuck out his hand and introduced himself.

Sophie had to give him credit for remaining unflappable about the whole situation. But then David was always unflappable. It was one of his best qualities. Watching the two men shake hands, she couldn't help but be struck by their contrasting appearances. David with his smoothly combed silver hair and sharp patrician features; Grant, rugged and handsome, wearing jeans and an obscenely tight collared jersey. One looked the perfect lawyer, which of course he was. The other looked...

Dangerous. With his pheromones and the way he demanded attention even in the most crowded and open of spaces. There was no better other word. He made David, whose long, lean frame stood the exact same height, look small.

To her embarrassment, she'd missed what David had said.

"Sophie?"

"What?"

"I asked if you wanted to bring your briefcase inside. We have a little while before we need to leave for the fundraiser. I thought I could beg a cocktail off you."

"Certainly easier than going out for one. I'm sure she has a fully stocked bar," Grant remarked drily.

Sophie felt another flush of warmth, this time exacerbated by David's perplexed expression. Bending, she retrieved her briefcase from where she dropped it when climbing into the tub. Thankfully David hadn't seen her doing that. "I wouldn't mind a few moments to freshen up," she said, changing the topic.

"If you'd like, but you look fine to me."

"I have to agree," Grant chimed in. He turned to David. "If you'd like, while you're waiting you can help me with the tub. The extra set of hands could come in handy."

"I would, but I'm not really dressed for the job," David replied.

"That's all right. If the deliverymen don't show up, Sophie's already said she'll take my phone call. Isn't that right, Sophie?"

He'd dropped his voice on purpose. Sophie narrowed her eyes.

Meanwhile, David was frowning again. "I'm afraid I don't understand."

"Never mind. I'll explain it to you inside." Turning her back on the grinning contractor, she hooked her arm in David's, leading him up the steps. "Right after I turn off my phone."

* * *

"I'm confused," David repeated once Sophie closed her front door. "I thought you said your neighbor shut the door in your face."

"He did. We've buried the hatchet, so to speak." Although if he kept it up, the hatchet might not stay buried for long. Bad enough Grant seemed to enjoy pushing her buttons so much, but did she have to react so easily? Every comment, every look, every touch. Her body was still overheated from their conversation earlier. "In fact, he's the one who fixed my water problem."

"I thought you said it was a plumber," David said, still frowning and watching Grant through the front windows. Sophie tapped him on the shoulder and motioned for him to follow her to the kitchen.

"It was, but Grant was the one who called him. He's a contractor—historical renovator, really," she corrected automatically, "and the plumber was one of his contacts."

"Oh, I see. But why was he making jokes about you having a well-stocked bar?"

"He's been making fun of that since he had dinner here the other night. Pizza," she added for David's scowl's benefit. "After he looked at the pipes."

She poured him a glass of Pinot Grigio. "It's a long and complicated story. I could have sworn I told you all this."

"Must have slipped your mind with all the work," David offered, accepting the glass.

"Must have," she agreed, putting the bottle on the counter with a guilty thud. The memory of how she almost kissed Grant in this very room weighed heavily on her.

"Turns out Grant worked on this building when it was being converted into co-ops," she said. "I'm thinking of having him do some work on my kitchen."

There. Couldn't say she didn't disclose that piece of information.

"You sure that's a good idea?" David asked.

After the tub business a few minutes ago, no. Somehow, though, she didn't think that's what David meant. "Why wouldn't it be?"

"What do you know about him? I mean the man's got a bathtub on your sidewalk. How do you know if he's even reliable?"

"Just because the man bought a tub from a junk dealer doesn't make him a bad contractor." One thing for her to have doubts; she didn't think David needed to get all high-and-mighty or insult her decision making process.

"It's hardly the first time I've hired someone," she added. "I think I'm capable of discerning whether or not the man can add a window properly."

"I'm sorry," David replied. "You're absolutely right. He threw me with all that nonsense about late-night phone calls. If I didn't know better, I'd say he was flirting with you."

"No," Sophie said. "That's just his way. I think he thinks it's charming." Not to mention as sexy as hell.

"Well, I know you'll make a careful decision. You're nothing if not levelheaded."

"Thank you." After how easily her resolve melted on the sidewalk, she wondered. Still she offered David her warmest smile. She had enough talking—and thinking—about her hot man-child neighbor for the day. Time to focus on the man she should be focused on. The one standing across from her.

The one who didn't make her kitchen feel tight and narrow.

"The delivery guys showed up right after they went inside," Grant relayed later that evening. "Good thing. I would have felt like a moron sitting on the edge of my tub waving goodbye. Probably would have said some smart-mouthed comment, too, just to see her reaction." He'd developed a thing for the way her cheeks flooded with color. Better looking than any cosmetic.

Next to him, Nate Silverman sat propped in his hospital bed, eyes aimed at the game playing out on his TV. On the screen, a ball passed the diving shortstop's glove.

"Tampa's been hot lately. Bet they make a run in September. Your Sox better watch out."

He sat back in the green leather chair and fiddled with the stitching along the arm. "The guy Sophie was going out with? Complete corporate shill. You remember the type. Designer suit, three-hundred-dollar shoes." The way they used to dress, only with silver hair. Wonder if he made Sophie blush deeply, too?

An odd, angry tightness gripped his chest at the thought. "Bet he's dull," he said aloud to Nate. "He looked it."

No, he looked exactly the way he expected a guy Sophie would date to look. She no doubt had a whole checklist of predetermined qualities. Wasn't that something someone with a master plan would do?

"I really don't know why I'm so fascinated with her. Besides the fact she's gorgeous. I think it's because..." His gaze grew distant. "You know the idea that people cross your path for a reason?" Something drew him to her. The answer lay right in front of him, too, only he couldn't see it. What else was new. He was good at being blind to what stood right before his eyes. "Maybe I'm supposed to show her how to loosen up." Or maybe she was here to remind him. To keep him from screwing up again.

"Did I tell you I started designing her kitchen? Dragged out the old CADD program and everything." Because she wanted a new room. "Scary how easy it is to get lost in the work again. Remember the buzz you could get when a design idea clicked? I forgot how addictive that feeling could be."

His choice of words made him wince. "Sorry, pal. Didn't mean to bring up a sore topic." The feeling he described was from a long time ago. Before Nate started chasing a different kind of buzz, one that he, lost in a chase of his own, failed to notice.

A petite woman with short brown hair appeared in the doorway. "It's getting late, Mr. Templeton. Nate needs to get ready for bed."

"Sure thing. We were just wrapping up." Grant rose to his feet. He stretched his arms high over his head and stretched. The soft crack of his vertebrae coming back into line echoed in the quiet. "Sorry to spend the whole visit gnawing your ear off about Sophie. Next time I'll focus more on the game. Promise."

Guilt rising in his throat, the way it did every visit, Grant reached down and patted the dark-haired man's shoulders. Nate didn't respond. But then he never did. The Nate he knew departed this world two years ago, leaving only the shell behind. A bedridden reminder of what was and what could have been.

And would never be again, thanks to Grant.

CHAPTER SIX

SINCE the day she left home twenty-two years earlier, Sophie dedicated Saturday mornings to doing three tasks: doing her laundry, cleaning her apartment and paying her bills. She was halfway through the third chore when the clanging started.

"You've got to be kidding," she said, tossing her ballpoint down. Grant's tub had been delivered. What on earth was he doing now? Images of him bent over, smacking on pipes with a wrench came to mind. The hem of his shirt would be pulled up ever so slightly, the way it did whenever he bent down, showing that sliver of tanned back. Or, perhaps the heat made him skip the T-shirt altogether and his muscular arms glistened slick with perspiration.

Nice, Sophie. Objectify the guy like one of the dirty old executives you read about in the tab-

loids. Though if her mind did insist on going down the objectifying road—again—Grant shared part of the blame. He was the one who talked about bathing on the sidewalk.

Still, she might as well see how long the racket would last. After all, if Grant intended on disrupting another one of her Saturday afternoons, she wanted to know.

That was the only reason she headed upstairs. It had nothing to do with curiosity regarding his attire. Absolutely nothing.

Grant opened the door on the second round of knocking. He was, to her disappointment, wearing a regular old T-shirt. "Let me guess," he greeted, folding his arms, "you're here about the clanging, right? I'm disturbing you and your friend?"

She took a moment to understand his implication. "David isn't here."

"Sorry to hear that," Grant replied.

"No need. We, that is, I…" She didn't have to explain anything to the man. "I came upstairs to find out if you planned on making noise all day like last time."

"Interrupting work again am I?"

The sarcasm wasn't any more entertaining today than it was last weekend, despite their truce. "I'm trying to pay my bills at the moment, but yes, later I have to work."

"Stock market's not in session."

A throwback to the other night when she told him she worked when the markets were open. "Maybe not, but I still am."

"No rest for the weary, eh?"

Weary was what she felt. Thanks to him. "You haven't answered my question. Are you going to be making noise all weekend?"

"Actually, you'll be happy to know I'm almost finished. In fact, I'm about to hook up the final piece. Want to come in and see the finished product?"

"I…" Remembering all the sordid images having taken residence in her head, she should decline. "I don't think so."

"Why not?"

Because I got cozy with you on a public sidewalk and spent way too much time focusing on what your skin tastes like. Lord knows what I'll do inside your apartment. "I have to get back to my bills."

"The bills will wait. Come on in. You know you're curious."

"No, I'm not," she started to lie, only to have him take her hand and pull her through the threshold. "Okay, maybe just a moment."

Grant's apartment was like the man himself: original, masculine and gorgeous. The narrow living room/dining area had many of the same features as her apartment. The fireplace had the same intricately carved woodwork for example. But despite the similarities, the room managed to have a personality all of its own. A granite island let light into the kitchen. She looked through with envy at the cabinets and stainless steel appliances.

"Do all the other apartments look like this?" she asked, thinking Etta should have been a little less stubborn.

"No, they're far more modern. In fact, you go to the top floors and you won't believe you're in the same building.

"The place was designed for selling," he added in a jaded-sounding voice. The tone didn't suit him.

"I've been trying to bring back as much of the original as possible. Can't completely turn back the hands of time, but I do what I can."

From the looks, he'd done a lot. The windows, the woodwork, all looked original, only in better condition. Decorating-wise, Grant apparently leaned toward bachelor sparseness. He was obviously more interested in structural details than curtains. There was a built-in bookcase actually filled with books, a plasma TV and a comfortable-looking leather sofa. A drafting table piled high with papers and reference books sat next to the doorway. There was also a large coffee table, which, from the looks of things, served double duty as a dining room table. Sophie noticed a coffee cup and two empty beer bottles holding down the newspaper. The entire room had been painted beige and brown adding to the masculine feel.

Sophie eyed the front windows with their beige trim. "Painted woodwork?" She arched a brow. "Aren't you breaking your own rule?"

"It's pine."

"Oh."

"Nice to know you paid attention, though."

Actually she hadn't. If she recalled, she'd been busy watching his hands. However, the lesson appeared to have made its way through to her brain nonetheless.

She strolled over to study the print hanging on his back wall. A black-and-white photo of Manhattan's Flatiron Building. Man liked his buildings, didn't he? "I imagine if your old neighbor saw all this work, she'd be impressed."

"Maybe. I'm not renovating to impress anyone, though."

"Why are you?"

"Because the house shouldn't have been torn up in the first place." His answer was uncharacteristically clipped. So much so, Sophie actually stepped back.

Seeing the reaction, his voice softened a little. Only a little, though. "Etta was pushed into the conversion," he explained.

"I thought you said she was afraid the place would get gutted after she died."

"Someone had to put the thought in her head, didn't they?" And from the sound of his voice, he didn't like that person very much, either. "Since I moved in twenty-eight months ago, I've been working to put the place back the way it was."

Twenty-eight months. According to the Realtor, the co-ops didn't go on the market that much before, meaning he'd been renovating almost since the building was converted. A lot of effort for a man who worked on the original construction. Clearly he felt quite strongly about Etta being wronged.

"Want some coffee?" Grant asked her. "I was about to pour myself a cup when you knocked."

"Sure." After all, to say no would be rude, right?

She followed him to his kitchen, only to stop in front of an interesting wood cabinet tucked in the corner. Narrow and chipped, it had a small, carved door halfway down and what looked like a drop-down cabinet on the bottom.

"An antique phone cabinet," Grant told her when she asked. "I found it at the flea market on Thirty-fifth Street this past winter and decided it was too cool to resist. Guess you can say I'm a sucker for older, beautiful things."

His gaze, while he spoke, pinned her straight to the spot. All of a sudden the narrow hall got very warm and cramped. "You wouldn't have water instead, would you?" Sophie asked, rubbing down the prickles on the back of her neck.

Grant arched a brow, but didn't comment. "I'll see if I can rustle something up."

While he went to the fridge, she hovered in the door frame, preferring the distance. When he bent over, she forced her eyes not to search for the sliver of skin.

"Did you and your 'friend' have a good evening?" she heard him ask.

"His name is David, and yes, we did."

"Where'd you go? Fundraiser, right?"

"Yes." She shifted from one foot to another. "Are you really interested?" Talking about David with him made her nervous.

"No," Grant replied, back in her space. "I'm trying to be polite. So you went to a fundraiser," he prompted as he handed her a water bottle.

"At the Natural History Museum. It was a

networking event. One hundred and fifty law-
yers and their spouses mingling under the T. rex
bones."

"Sounds scintillating. The networking I mean."

"David found it useful."

"Did you?"

"Not really. It was David's event," she murmured, only to bite her lip when she realized
she'd admitted it aloud. "I mean our main purpose in going was to help David's career."

"Aren't you a good girlfriend."

Sophie's head shot up. "I'm not—"

"Not what?" he asked, brown eyes probing.
"Good or his girlfriend?"

The doorknob pressed into the small of her
back. She'd pressed herself so tightly against the
door she expected to see the facet pattern im-
printed on her skin. The correct response would
be to tell him David was her boyfriend. They
were dating, after all, and by admitting it, she
could put an end to Grant's continual flirting.

Instead, she propelled herself away from the
door and back into the main room. "Where is this
infamous bathroom? That's what I came to see."

"Come with me." He motioned for her to join him in a doorway a few feet way. Sophie found a bold graphic gray, black and white tile. The tub sat invitingly along the back wall, beneath a small built-in shelf. "It's gorgeous," Sophie said. "Though, aren't you going to miss having a real shower?" The tub had a handheld attachment.

"I still have a real shower, in the master bathroom," he replied, his voice coming from over her shoulder. "You didn't think I planned to bathe in this every night, did you?"

"I did have my questions." The image he suggested of him bathing naked on the sidewalk still hadn't left her brain yet.

"I suppose I can see how I might have given you the impression. But trust me, this baby is strictly for show." He paused what he was doing to look up at her. "Or company."

Sophie looked to her shoes. Company was not a good replacement image. It conjured up too many pictures of wet skin and strong arms wrapped around her waist. Particularly with his breath tickling her ear.

"So, do you like it?"

She started, mainly because his breath tickled her earlobe just as she got to a particularly steamy image. "Like what?"

"My apartment."

Right, his apartment. "Told you, the room is gorgeous. You definitely have…" At that moment, he leaned over and adjusted the towel that was hanging on a nearby towel ring. Peppermint and coffee teased her nostrils. "…skills," she managed to squeak out.

"Interesting choice of words."

Sophie shook her head. Damn if his arrogance wasn't appealing. And damn if his big broad chest wasn't brushing against her back. Took a second, but she managed to make her feet move and break their bodies' connection. "You need to work on your self-confidence," she told him.

Having delivered her comment, Sophie waited for the man to move so she could pass. Their various configurations of entering and exiting rooms were almost like a dance, weren't they? Draw close, separate. Professional and mature one moment, blushing and covered with goose bumps the next.

Distracted as she was with her thoughts, Sophie didn't see the drafting table until her thigh connected with its corner. The collision jostled the table, sending the mile-high pile of books and papers onto the floor.

"Are you all right?" Grant asked.

"Fine." She was more embarrassed about making a mess. "Let me help you pick this up."

"That's all right. You don't have to..."

Sophie's eyes widened at the titles strewn about her feet. *The Synthesis of Form. Traditional Details for Renovation and Rehabilitation. Form, Space and Order.* She glanced up. "Little light reading?"

"I was looking something up."

"You've got some hardcore resource materials." No wonder he knew so much about historical buildings. He obviously studied them. "Are you taking a class?"

"Did." He yanked the book she was holding from her hand. "Long time ago."

Couldn't have been that long ago. He wasn't old enough. "In college?"

"Why does it matter where I took the class?"

"I was just curious. I apologize." She of all people should respect a person's desire for privacy about even the most benign of subjects.

Unless said subjects involved her. A sketch that had fallen on the floor caught her eye. It was a computer drawing of a kitchen. A very familiar kitchen.

"Is this my place?" she asked, reaching for the paper. Sure enough, there was her kitchen, complete with the changes Grant described the other day. "Did you draw these?"

"Just something I was fooling around with."

"Your fooling around looks pretty impressive. Professional."

"Four years of Columbia architecture school will do that for you." He snatched the drawing from her hand, causing it to tear in two.

Sophie barely noticed. "You're an architect?" An Ivy League educated one at that.

"Was." Grant's face had grown so dark and grim you'd think she'd accused him of a crime. Same with the sour way he spoke. "Not anymore. I quit twenty-eight months ago."

Around the same time he moved in. After the

building had been converted. But he said he'd met Etta during the time the conversion took place.

Suddenly it dawned on her. "When you said you met the owner…"

"I designed the building."

The man who turned the place modern even though it should never have been "cut up," to use Grant's words. The man that twenty minutes earlier she'd have sworn he held in contempt.

"What happened?" she asked in a soft voice. "Were you the one who convinced her to break up the building?"

Grant didn't answer. Dropping the drawing on his desk, he walked to his windows. In the bright summer light, his figure became a black silhouette. Large and brooding. Seeing him was enough of an answer. He had been the man he described so angrily earlier.

Sophie moved to join him. Yes, she should honor his privacy, but he looked so pained she couldn't help wanting to reach out. Why was he converting the place back again?

She was two steps from his shoulder when he spoke. "I have to see a vendor at the flea market about some lighting fixtures," he said, face still focused outside.

"Okay," Sophie replied. He didn't want to talk. She would take the hint. Respect it. "I'll get back to my—"

"Come with me."

He spun around so quickly she nearly stumbled. "What?"

"It's too beautiful a day to spend stuck inside. Come with me."

"I can't. I have to work."

There was an energy behind his invitation that she couldn't name. What did it matter if she accompanied him or not? Sophie was having trouble keeping her balance from the mood swings. She wished she could name the energy she sensed coming off him. Not for the first time she wondered if his enthusiasm was stronger than necessary. *What are you trying to avoid, Grant Templeton?*

"The work will be there when you get back."

Sure, along with a whole lot more, knowing Allen. "I really can't."

"Yes, you can," he insisted, closing the last couple of steps between them and tucking a finger underneath her chin. "You know you want to."

"So, you're a mind reader now?" The response might have worked better if her jaw wasn't quivering from his touch.

"Not a mind reader," he returned. "Eye reader. And yours are saying an awful lot."

Forced enthusiasm or not, his touch was making her insides quiver. She wanted desperately to look away and refuse to make eye contact with him, but pride wouldn't let her. Instead, she forced herself to keep her features as bland as possible so he wouldn't see that a part of her—the very female part—did want to go with him. It also wanted to feel more of his touch, too, and the common sense part of her was having a hard time forming an opposing argument.

"If so, then no doubt you know they're saying, 'remove your hand.'"

He chuckled. Soft and low. *A bedroom laugh.* "Did you know they flash when you're being stubborn?"

Rather than argue, Sophie swallowed her pride and looked to his feet. That only earned her another maddening chuckle. "You so don't want me to move my hand, either."

"You're incorrigible. You know that, right?"

"Thank you."

"I still want you to move your hand."

"If you insist...." Suddenly his hands were cupping her cheeks, drawing her parted lips under his. Sophie's gasp was lost in her throat. As she expected, he tasted of peppermint and coffee and...and...

And oh, Lord, could he kiss!

It ended and her eyelids fluttered open. Grant's face hovered a breath from hers. Gently, he traced the slope of her nose and smiled.

"Your eyes told me you wanted that, too."

If she had an ounce of working brain matter, Sophie would have turned and stormed out of his apartment then and there. Problem was one, she was trembling, and two, the fact she'd kissed him back probably wiped out any outrage she'd be trying to convey.

So she did the next best thing. She folded her arms across her chest and presented him with a somewhat flushed but indignant expression. "Do not do that again."

"Do what? Kiss you?"

"Yes, kiss me," she snapped back. His smug smile upped her indignity. "I don't care what you *think* you saw in my eyes, it's not appropriate, and I'm not interested."

He didn't even have the dignity to look chagrined. "I don't know about inappropriate," he drawled, "but you and I both know you're lying about not being interested."

Arrogant, overconfident, caramel-eyed… Before she could finish the thought, he'd wrapped his hand in hers and was leading her toward the door. "Come on," he said, pausing only to pick up his wallet from off the coffee table. "You can lock your door on the way out."

And that was how Sophie came to be mutely escorted down her front steps and across the street.

"Loosen up, Sophie. You look like you're being held prisoner."

Wasn't she? Sophie looked at the hand that had clasped hers since Grant led her from the apartment. His large fingers entwined with hers, gently and loosely. She could pull away anytime she wanted. The one holding on was her.

"Ever been to the flea market before?" Grant asked, ignoring when she let go and stuffed her fist in her shorts pocket.

"No."

"You're in for an experience."

She wasn't sure she wanted another experience. Her fingers were tingling and her insides had become a big ball of confusion from the last one. Only yesterday she'd given herself a long lecture about decorum and professionalism and what have you, and what did she do? Let Grant kiss her. Kiss him back. Then, instead of doing the sensible thing and refusing to go with him, here she was strolling along as if they were on a date!

Her briefcase at home was filled with pressing work. With the day ticking by, she had absolutely no business traipsing about the city under any circumstances, let alone traipsing about with a man a decade younger than she was. No matter how romantic and enigmatic he seemed to be. And, since when did she use words like *romantic* and *enigmatic,* anyway?

To make matters truly bad, her lips could still feel Grant's kiss, and her body really, really wanted another.

Beside her, Grant nudged her shoulder with his. "I promise, the world won't stop because you took a few hours off."

"Easy for you to say. You weren't kidnapped and forced to go against your will."

"Forced to spend a beautiful summer's day outside. How horrible!" He clutched his chest in mock horror. "There's no need to be dramatic. You had plenty of opportunities to reject any or all of my advances. If I recall, you didn't put up much of a fight."

No, she hadn't, unfortunately. Hard to when you're dazed and dizzy. "Why did you kiss me?" she asked him.

"I told you, because your eyes said to." He grinned. "Along with certain parts of my body."

Sophie was not amused. "I'm serious, Grant. You've been flirting with me for days now and I want to know why."

"All right." His expression sobered. "Because you're a beautiful woman, and I'm attracted to you. Satisfied?"

No. "I'm a decade older than you are."

"Big deal. I don't give a rat's behind about age. You could be two decades older and I'd still find you attractive. And," he continued, preempting her by wagging a finger, "before you go talking about how it's unprofessional, it was one kiss. If you don't want me to kiss you again, say so and I won't."

"I don't want you to kiss me again."

"Liar."

Oh, for crying out loud! "This is a bad idea. I'm going back." She started to turn only to feel him grip her at the elbow.

"Relax. You have my word I'll be on my best behavior. No more kissing."

"Promise?"

"Absolutely. Unless you ask me to, of course," he added in the slow-honeyed drawl she'd come to love and despise.

Sophie wanted to kill him. "Grant…"

"Scout's honor."

Freeing her arm from his grip, she scowled, her displeasure aimed at the actual manhandling than the part of her that regretted making the deal. "You better be as good a Boy Scout as you claimed you were," she muttered.

The flea market entrance ended the conversation. Seeing the crowds, Sophie had to blink. She'd known bargain hunting was popular, but she'd had no idea how much so. This place was filled with shoppers, hundreds of them, all jammed around a collection of vendors and tables. From what she could tell, a person could find almost anything if they were patient and looked hard enough. She saw pottery, clothes, tools. There was even a row of vendors selling fresh food.

"I can't believe you've never been here," Grant said.

"Not much of a secondhand person," she replied. At least not now that she could afford first-hand.

"You've been missing out." Reaching into his back pocket, he took out a folded vendor map. "My guy is at table W-64. Over here."

They wound the row of tents of vintage clothes, antiques, crafts and other items. Grant, of course, insisted on guiding her with his hand splayed annoyingly close to the small of her back. He might as well have been touching her, for the warmth it caused.

Making matters worse was the fact it took forever for them to reach their destination. Even amidst the throng, vendors recognized Grant and would call him over to their table. Each time Sophie would find herself watching while Grant chatted them up, about items they wanted to show him, about items he might have purchased previously, or simply about innocuous topics like sports.

"You've got quite the network," she commented.

"Have to. Half the challenge of historical renovation is finding the exact right piece for a job."

"Is that why you got into the business? For the challenge?"

"Sort of" was his reply. A variation on "we'll see." "Might as well bring back to life what I can. There's my guy."

Grant's vendor was in the corner, between a

vintage clothing dealer and a man selling personalized street signs. Soon as he saw them, he limped to the back of the tent and dragged out a large box of what looked like, to Sophie, a pile of lamp shades and wires. Grant knew what they were, though. He immediately knelt down and began sorting through the items. Leaning against a rack of fur coats, she watched as he examined each piece, ultimately returning or discarding based on results. Occasionally the vendor would pipe up with information, but it was obvious the show was all Grant's.

He was an enigma, that's for certain. It would be so easy to write him off as a flirtatious stud, but the title didn't completely fit. Behind the sexy smile and perfect-looking features lived a layer of deep emotion. A bleakness that held her interest in a far stronger grip than his looks. Something happened twenty-eight months ago that clearly affected him deeply. What?

"Hard to resist, huh?"

Sophie found a chic, perfumed woman in a strapless sundress standing next to her.

"Nineteen-fifties. Very Audrey Hepburn." She

reached into the rack to remove the fur and blue brocade coat whose sleeve Sophie had absent-mindedly grabbed hold of while watching Grant. "You want to try it on?"

"No, thanks. I don't do vintage clothing. I'm merely killing time waiting for my…" Oh, goodness, she was tripping over the word *friend* again.

She shouldn't. Friend is what Grant was.

"But the color would look great on you," the vendor persisted. Before Sophie could protest, the woman had the coat off the rack and was thrusting it in her direction. "Go on. If you like it I'll give you a good price."

"No, I don't think—" Sophie was about to press the coat back in the woman's arms when the sun caught the gold-green thread on the brocade, making the cloth look almost metallic. She didn't know about Audrey Hepburn, but it was pretty….

"Okay," she acquiesced. She might as well. If Grant heard the discussion he'd only come over and badger her until she did.

She slipped her arms into the sleeves. The cloth

smelled like mothballs and the thick extra layer made the summer heat more oppressive than ever.

"Nice," the woman said with a smile. A few feet away a vanity mirror rested against an old coat tree. She angled the glass so Sophie could see her reflection.

Well, what do you know? She didn't look as foolish as she thought. In fact, the coat actually did look…nice. More than nice. It looked good. The cape style coat swung around her knees and, when she pulled the front plackets closed, the fur collar framed her chin perfectly.

"Wow! Sexy," a male voice said from behind her.

The open appreciation ran along her spine, warming her even more than the coat. "Thank you," she said, giving her reflection another admire before slipping the coat off. She placed it back on the rack.

Grant stepped into view. "You're not getting it?"

"Vintage clothing doesn't exactly fit with my lifestyle. I can only imagine the looks I'd get walking down Wall Street."

"Too bad. Could have been a new you."

"I'll stick to the old me, if you don't mind."

"If you say so," Grant replied. It was an innocuous enough comment. So why did Sophie suddenly feel as though she failed a test?

Changing the subject, she asked, "Are you finished with your business already?" She noticed he held only a small plastic shopping bag. "Your bag doesn't look big enough to hold light figures. Didn't he have what you were looking for?"

"Most of the stuff needed too much fixing to be worth my while. A couple of brass fixtures. Oh, and a few hinges to replace the one I saw was coming loose in your kitchen."

"Wait a minute. Back up. You bought a hinge for my cabinet?"

"A couple actually. Remember I mentioned yours needed replacing."

"Thank you."

"No big deal. I saw them and realized they matched your kitchen, so I grabbed them."

Perhaps he didn't see it as a big deal, but to Sophie it was an unexpected, odd, kind gesture.

An inexplicable warmth spread through her. "Does this mean I owe you again?"

"We'll see." He cocked his head. "You ready for lunch?"

Sophie nodded. She gave the coat another last look and felt the queerest pull. A kind of longing or feeling of desperate want.

Don't be silly, she told herself. *It's just an old coat.*

CHAPTER SEVEN

REMNANTS of that strange sensation dogged Sophie long after they left the flea market and resumed walking. She simply couldn't shake the feeling she was missing out on something. It was a nagging uneasiness at the back of her brain, much like the feeling you got when you left the iron plugged in. Which was probably why she barely noticed until they sat down that the restaurant Grant had steered her toward was several blocks in the opposite direction of their apartment building. A small sidewalk bistro near Grand Army Plaza with tables shaded by linden trees.

Grant leaned back in his chair, sunlight and shadows dappling his hair. "Isn't this better than spending the afternoon inside doing paperwork?" he asked as a waitress served them tall glasses of iced tea she didn't remember ordering.

"I guess." Now that they were seated, the briefcase full of work had resumed nagging her. How much time had she wasted? She took out her BlackBerry to check.

Unfortunately, she couldn't tell, because no sooner did she find her phone then Grant's hand reached across and closed over hers, preventing her from looking at its face.

"Put it away," he told her. "This is a cell phone free lunch."

"I'm only checking the time."

"Why? Got hot plans for tonight? With your friend David maybe?" He blew the paper from his straw, aiming it like a missile in her direction.

"No, I don't have plans with David," she replied, batting away the paper with her free hand. "He's on his way to Chicago for a business trip." Actually, he had suggested last night they meet today for an early dinner, but she'd begged off claiming work. Work she hadn't got done because her neighbor had kidnapped her.

"If you don't have plans, you don't need your phone."

"I—" Did his grip have to be so...so solid?

"No arguments. It's a beautiful afternoon. Put your phone away and enjoy yourself. That's an order."

"I didn't realize you were in command," she muttered, angry with herself over how easily she capitulated. He had this uncanny ability to get her to do what he wanted. "Do you boss all your lunch companions around like this?"

"Only the pretty workaholics."

"You do realize that all you've succeeded in doing is making me work twice as late when we get home. Instead of being stuck inside Saturday afternoon, I'll be working Saturday night."

"Unless I distract you tonight, too."

He could, too. Quite easily. That was the problem. "You mean to tell me a man like you doesn't have plans on a Saturday night?" She sat back in her seat. "And you tease me about not having a life."

"What makes you think I don't have plans?"

"You just said you'd distract me."

"So you do want me to distract you."

"I didn't say that." Even though the thought sent shivers down her spine. She repeated her question. "Do you have plans?" If he did, perhaps she could shake the spell he seemed to have over her.

"The only plans I have involve enjoying the company of a very attractive woman." He raised his glass. "I'm curious, though. What did you mean by 'a man like me'?"

Sophie blushed deep from both the compliment and the question. So much for breaking the spell. Keep this up and she'd have to start telling people she had a sunburn.

"Have you seen our waitress?" she asked, ignoring the question. "I'd like to order so we can get back. I've been 'distracted' enough for one day."

"Honey, we've barely started." With a shake of his head, he handed her a copy of the one page menu for her to review. "Someone's got to teach you how to stop and smell the roses."

A job for which he clearly appeared to have volunteered. Question was why? "Why do you care?"

He was sipping his iced tea. "What can I say? I believe in rescuing damsels in distress. I hate to see a woman spend her days locked in her office toiling away at financial figures when she could be out enjoying herself in the sunshine."

"I appreciate the concern." But she didn't fully buy the explanation. She'd caught the way his smile faltered slightly when she asked. "Is that the only reason?" she pressed.

"You think there's more?"

"Uh-huh." Definitely. The more she thought about it, the more she became convinced his flirting and continual interest in distracting her *had* to have a catch. She simply wasn't that fascinating.

Sipping her drink, she watched and waited. With the tables turned, her young companion had lost a bit of his swagger. A part of her found pleasure in that. He was cute when he squirmed. The way he fiddled with the edge of the menu. How his brow furrowed as he tried to think of a smart answer. Definitely cute. If cute came in a big, sexy, virile package.

At last, he stopped his fiddling. "If you must know," he said, "you remind me of someone."

"Who?" She held up her hand. "Let me guess— your father."

He laughed. "Why on earth would you suggest him?"

"You already told me I don't remind you of your mother. Figured I'd try the other side of the family tree."

"You don't remind me of either of my parents," he told her.

"Good to know. Though I'm certainly old enough to be one of them," she added over the edge of her straw.

"Why do you do that?"

"Do what?"

"Keep referring to how you're older than me."

"How about because I am." One of them had to remember.

"So what? I happen to like old, remember?"

Old and beautiful. She remembered. "I thought that only applied to building materials."

"It applies to a lot of things."

"Oh." She took a long sip of her tea to quell the jumble in her stomach. Unlike a lot of his answers, this one hadn't come with any suggestive tone or innuendo, though you'd think from her sudden bout of shy uncertainty that it had.

Feeling the unsettledness from before rising upward, she scrambled to regain control of herself and the conversation. "If I don't remind you of your parents, who do I remind you of?"

His face crinkled in thought. "That's just it. I'm not entirely sure. But you definitely remind me of someone.

"Besides myself, that is," he added in a lower voice. He'd raised the menu as he spoke so she couldn't see his features to know if the comment was meant to be flirtatious. His tone suggested otherwise.

"I remind you of you? How?" They couldn't be more different.

For the first time, the tables were truly turned and color tinged his cheeks. "Did I say that aloud?"

"Very much so. And now I'm dying to know how we're alike."

"Let's say I used to have a cell phone glued to my hands, too."

An incomplete answer and an intriguing one for when he spoke, the sadness returned to his eyes. He tried to hide the expression behind his menu, but Sophie caught it nonetheless.

"And you consider that habit a bad one."

"In my experience, tunnel vision of any kind is a bad habit."

Moving her drink and menu aside, Sophie leaned forward and prodded. "What experience?"

"Are you ready to order?"

Damn the waitstaff in the place. Efficient and invisible. Their waitress reappeared like a specter, her notepad in hand. Sophie could feel Grant's relief. Whatever experience, she could tell it hadn't been pleasant. She didn't like how the memory distressed him. She much preferred his smile. His warm, sexy smile.

The waitress took their orders and disappeared as quickly and efficiently as she arrived. Without a menu to fiddle with, Grant quickly turned to his silverware for distraction, making a large production out of aligning his salad and dinner forks.

"Did you know our building has a secret passage?" he asked suddenly.

His attempt to dodge the subject at hand

worked. Sophie was distracted. "Like a tunnel? Are you sure?"

"I know the building inside and out. Of course I'm sure. And we're talking a stairway, not tunnel."

Still fascinating. "Why build a secret anything? Were they bootleggers or part of the Underground Railroad?" The house was old enough to have seen both Prohibition and the Civil War.

"Nothing so romantic," he replied. The waitress materialized and wordlessly set down their salads. "A lot of houses built during the era had back staircases so the servants could travel between floors without being seen."

"Shoot. Here I thought I'd bought into a historic landmark. Where are these stairs? I never noticed any place that would hide them."

"Behind your pantry wall. The original kitchen is now our basement. There was a set of steps running from the ground floor to the roof. The top flights came down during renovation, but since the two flights from garden level to the second floor were already boarded up, we left them. Another one of Etta's insistences."

Good for her. Sophie picked up her fork and dug into her salad. "Are they usable? That is, if you knocked the wall down?" She thought of all the times as a kid she could have used a hidden passage. A place to disappear when real life got too crazy.

"Why? You interested in making a midnight visit to my bedroom?"

Cheeks hotter than Hades—because the notion put some way too appealing images in her head—Sophie stabbed at her salad. Figures the waitress couldn't materialize now when an interruption would be useful.

"Don't get any ideas," she warned.

"Too late," he replied, spearing his own tomato. "The idea has already been firmly planted in my brain. First thing tomorrow I'm getting out the sledgehammer and knocking down the walls. And you won't be able to complain about the banging because you suggested the idea."

"Then I'll install an alarm in the pantry."

"You mean those surplus boxes and cans stored in there won't be alarm enough?"

She tossed him a smirk. "They're to toss at unwanted visitors."

"Well, since you only throw them at unwanted visitors, I'm safe. What do you say, should I clear a path so I can come down and tuck you in?"

Sophie didn't think it was possible to flush more. "Must you turn every conversation sexual?"

"Can't help myself. You make me think sexual thoughts."

"Hardly." She rolled her eyes.

"I'm serious. Why do you find it so hard to believe that I'm attracted to you? You are a stunningly beautiful woman."

"Who is…"

"A decade older," he supplied. "As you've mentioned a decade worth of times. And since you feel the need to constantly put that out, it's only fair that I constantly remind you how desirable you are."

If it were only that simple, thought Sophie. But he was trying too hard, and she was beginning to see a pattern.

"Know what I think?" she asked, setting her fork down.

His reply was delayed by the well-timed arrival of their entrées. Sophie swore the restaurant was timing their efficiency for exactly those moments when she didn't want an interruption. She waited impatiently for the young woman to set each plate down.

"What I think," she continued when finally alone, "is that you're trying to distract me."

Grant swallowed the sweet potato fry he was chewing. "Distract you from what?"

Nice try. Repeating the question was a classic avoidance tactic. "My asking questions." Discussing the topic he so obviously wanted to avoid.

"You make it sound like I'm keeping secrets." His chuckle was low and nervous. She'd touched on a nerve.

"Are you?"

"Don't be ridiculous. I don't have any secrets to keep. What you see is what you get."

What Sophie saw was a man avoiding a painful memory. "All right then," she said, "if you don't have secrets, answer me this. Why did you quit architecture? Does it have something to do with Etta, the woman who used to own our building?"

He didn't answer. Instead he fiddled with his tableware, becoming inordinately interested in the clanking noise his knife made against the tiny pot of ketchup on his plate.

"Grant?"

"Not really," he replied, only to shrug and add, "Peripherally. I'm not proud of what happened with Etta, but it was only a symptom of a far bigger problem."

This time it was Sophie's hand reaching across and covering his. Her need to know had moved beyond curiosity. The reproach she heard him struggling to keep from his voice called out for comfort.

"What happened?" she asked him.

For a moment, from the way he stared mutely at their hands, she wondered if he'd dodge the topic again. When he did speak, the words are soft and laced with sorrow.

"I nearly killed my best friend."

* * *

Sophie's soft gasp told Grant he'd succeeded in shocking her.

"You're being dramatic, right?"

Maybe, a little. Mike would certainly say so. The hole in his gut argued differently. Of course, now that he'd made the admission, he would have to explain what happened. Why'd he say anything? He bit back a groan. Flirting was so much easier.

Pulling his hand free, he kept his fingers busy by plucking sesame seeds from the top of his burger bun. Where to start?

With the damn award. "Every year the Architect Association honors the city's top young architect. Winning can cement your career. Coming out of Columbia, my goal was to win. I had it all planned out. I'd score a job with a top firm, win the award, be proclaimed the city's next star-architect and become a millionaire before I turned thirty."

He offered her a wan smile. "My family believes in setting big goals."

"Nothing wrong with aiming high," Sophie replied.

Naturally the woman with a master plan would agree.

"Anyway," he continued with a sigh, "everything was falling into line. I had the job. I was making great money. All I needed was to blow the socks off the partners and the Architect Association."

"So far this all sounds quite admirable," Sophie remarked. "What does it have to do with your best friend?"

"I'm getting to that." Man, was he getting to it. His mouth had run dry so Grant reached for his iced tea. Why was telling this story so hard? He'd been telling himself he wanted Sophie to loosen up. To open her eyes to the dangers of closing yourself off to everything but work. This was his chance.

"Nate and I went to college together. We were roommates. More than roommates. Best friends. Competitive ones at that, not that there was much competition. He beat me at everything. Awards, grades. We spent four years with him being number one, and me being right behind at number two. He even scored his job first. With Kimeout, Hannah and Miller, the city's top firm."

Memories of Nate doing his job offer dance popped into his head, making him smile. *They want me; they want me.*

"Sounds like he was born under a lucky star," Sophie said.

"Like you wouldn't believe. Too bad the luck faded after graduation."

"What do you mean?"

He shrugged. "Design in theory and design in practice are two different things. Maybe he simply had bad chemistry with the partners, but Nate just couldn't seem to catch a break. Meanwhile I was determined to best him at something. I had to be number one."

"You mean winning the award."

The damn award. His holy grail. Grabbing his iced tea again, he drank down the knot in his throat. Guilt never tasted good. "I put everything I had into becoming the best, fastest rising architect this city had ever seen. I worked round the clock, did whatever it took. Even if that meant convincing an old woman her building would go co-op."

"Our building."

"Bingo. Our senior partner wanted the developer's business. I knew if I could score Etta's building, I'd earn major points." It was the beginning of his downward slide.

"That's why you're renovating? To make amends."

He nodded. It wasn't much, but it was something.

"And what about Nate? What happened there?"

"I told you, he was competitive and used to being the star. The more I pushed, the more he pushed, too. Except…"

"Except what?" Her hand was back, soft and comforting on his wrist.

"He couldn't keep up. I was so caught up in the competition—in winning—I didn't see the signs." This is where the story turned its bleakest. "He was edgy all the time. Moody. Unpredictable. His work was erratic. One day he'd be flying all over the office, next he'd zone out during an important meeting."

"He was using."

"Cocaine. He'd snorted the stupid stuff in college once or twice. Said it boosted his creativity. I had no idea things had gotten so out of hand." In hindsight, the evidence was so overwhelming. Making him feel even worse.

"You were focused on your own work. You didn't know."

Grant expected her to say as much. But, his focus had been the problem. "We had this huge blowout one afternoon. Nate accused me of trying to poach his project after he caught me talking to his client. The guy called me because he couldn't reach Nate."

"Reasonable enough."

So the lie Grant tried to sell himself said, as well. Only his heart knew he hadn't exactly discouraged the man from calling, either, and that he would have taken the project, if asked. That's how low he'd gone.

"The argument got pretty heated and the partners told him to take the rest of the day off. I should have known then." But he was too angry and caught up in getting Bob Kimeout's approval.

"I'm sorry," he heard Sophie say. Her thumb rubbed soft circles on the skin between his thumb and forefinger. The touch was soothing. More soothing than he deserved, but he didn't shake her off. "He called me that night. Nate. I was out for drinks with the partners, discussing my future. I let the phone go to voice mail. Figured we'd hash everything out in the morning."

He could see Nate's name on the call screen clear as day. Just one flick of his thumb and the ringer turned silent. One flick. He pictured the image until it grew blurry in his brain. "He collapsed that night. The coke stopped his heart."

Sophie gasped again. "Oh, my."

Grant stared at his plate. "I saw his name and I ignored him. My best friend." Remembering made him sick to his stomach. Now she knew. His eyes stayed on his plate, too afraid to look up and see the judgment in Sophie's eyes. She'd never look at him the same way again.

"It's not your fault," she said.

Why did people keep saying that to him? He'd become a man who turned off the phone when his best friend was in trouble. A man who didn't blink twice regarding anything, so long as it helped him get closer to his prize.

Might as well share the coup de grâce to his shame. "Want to know the kicker? I won the award. For my 'brilliantly designed blend of modern and historic.' Sound familiar? Congratulations to me." He raised his glass. "I quit the next day."

"Wow," Sophie said finally. "That's horrible." Sophie didn't know what more to say. What terrible regret for anyone to carry around. She was amazed the sadness in his eyes wasn't deeper, a testimony to how strong spirited he was. "I'm sorry for your loss."

"Wasn't my loss. It was Nate's."

No, it was both of theirs. Her chest ached. Like someone had sucker punched her breastbone. His story hit her in ways she hadn't expected. Yes, she felt his guilt and regret, yes, she empathized. Underneath the sympathy, however, she recognized a great realization. She felt as if she was truly seeing Grant for the very first time. The real Grant. Not her sexy younger neighbor, but a man. A flesh and blood man with a heavy soul and ghosts that could rival her own. A man a woman could easily fall for if she let herself.

A man who, like the flea market coat she put back on the rack, was all wrong for her.

Those thoughts dogged her the entire way home. Or rather they braided themselves with the sensation from the flea market leaving her insides all twisted. Since Grant wasn't doing a whole lot of talking, she had time to try and unravel them on the walk home. Unfortunately, all she could think of was how wrong the man was for her. There were so many reasons why, too. His age. The way he kept her off balance. His age.

The biggest issue, though, was the fact he simply did not fit into her plans. She wasn't looking for a fling; affairs weren't her style. And face it, what more could she do with Grant beyond a fling?

Plus, there was David, who was a far better fit for her lifestyle. Grant was simply some hot guy she'd known for a few days. Her feelings toward him were still mostly physical. The increased awareness, or whatever you want to call it, she was currently experiencing, meant nothing.

Glancing over, she saw that Grant remained lost in his own world. Regretting telling his story? Possibly. The muscle twitching in his jaw suggested as much.

"Thank you for lunch," she said, hoping to pull him from his reverie. "Or maybe I should say dinner. It's certainly late enough." Between the flea market and the restaurant, they managed to eat away a good portion of the day.

"Suppose this means you'll be up half the night working."

Sophie thought of the paperwork she left behind. "I did leave a lot unfinished. I hate unfinished business," she added softly. It reminded her too much of chaos. Of waiting for the next shoe to drop. She'd spent enough time waiting—and getting pegged by falling shoes—as a kid.

"My boss, Allen Breckinridge, tends to call at odd hours asking for information. Unfinished business means I have to scramble for a reason why I don't have the information he wants. Trust me, you never want to have to scramble in front of Allen Breckinridge."

"Breckinridge is the guy who kept calling the other night, right?"

"The one and the same. He's pretty sure the firm and the universe revolve around him. And, he expects perfection."

"I bet you give him perfection, too."

His tone didn't sound complimentary. Fallout from his confession no doubt. "I try." She didn't tell him about her fear of him waiting for her to make a mistake.

They'd reached their front door. Sophie fished out her keys, surprised to discover she was actually disappointed to be home. "I have to admit," she said, turning it in the lock, "as kidnappings go, this wasn't half bad."

"Careful, people might think Stockholm syndrome is setting in," Grant teased.

Falling for her kidnapper? Sophie smiled but didn't laugh. This was the Grant she'd come to expect, flirty and full of innuendo. Nonetheless, the joke hit a little too close to home. Her insides jumped at the thought. "Don't hold your breath."

"Tsk-tsk, such protest." Several strands of hair had worked their way loose from her ponytail. He smoothed them back from her cheek. Suddenly it was Sophie holding a breath. She held it while the fingertips traced her hairline, past her temple, over the shell of her ear and along her jaw. When he skimmed the curve of her neck, she had to choke back a sigh.

"What are you doing tomorrow?" he asked in that rough honey voice of his.

Sophie blinked. "Um, groceries." Took a moment, but she finally wracked her brain and remembered. "Sunday is grocery day. Why?"

"I thought I'd come by and fix those hinges."

"Hinges?" He was tracing the collar of her tank top now making it hard to concentrate. What was he up to? She'd told him not to kiss her again.

"Among other things. If you'd like, I could show you the secret passage."

Oh, but the suggestion sounded so wicked. "I'd like that."

"I'll see you tomorrow then." He leaned in just as his fingers reached her bare shoulder. "Good night, Sophie."

He was going to kiss her again. She held her breath again and waited.…

The other shoe never dropped.

Instead, with one last brush of his fingers across her cheek, Grant headed upstairs, leaving Sophie breathless, quivering and contemplating calling him back. Only the fact she lacked a working voice stopped her.

Dear Lord, she was in trouble.

CHAPTER EIGHT

NEXT morning found Sophie rescrubbing her kitchen with nervous energy. She'd already tackled the bathroom, not to mention reviewed the emails and reports she'd worked on until the middle of the night. Anything to keep her mind off yesterday's roller coaster ride with Grant.

Thing was, she didn't know what caused her insides to jumble more. That morning's kiss, the lack of a second kiss, or the emotional upheaval left by Grant's confession. It didn't matter. All three left her on edge.

The knock on the door made her stomach jump. "Coming!"

Quickly, she checked her appearance. She was wearing what she called her Saturday cleaning outfit: camisole, knee-length sweats and no makeup. Saturday's outfit on Sunday. Exactly what you'd expect a woman who wasn't in control to wear. At least her hair was combed. She readjusted the clip at the base of her neck, hoping she caught all the front strands and reached for the door.

It figured. With his hair mussed and morning stubble, Grant yet again looked as though he rolled off the pages of *Morning Sexy* magazine. In fact, the only flaw in his appearance was the circles under his eyes and even they looked good on him.

"Morning," Grant said. "I don't suppose you have coffee ready."

"Good morning to you, too," she greeted. "Late night?"

"Had trouble sleeping."

Join the club, she thought, closing the door behind him. Was he kicking himself for yesterday, too? She wasn't sure if she should be relieved or disappointed at the idea.

He was already in the kitchen when she pushed open the door. "Smells clean," he remarked to her. "Someone's been busy."

"I was up early with nothing to do." *Thanks to*

you. "I figured I might as well start fall cleaning a few months early."

"I'm surprised you aren't nose deep in paperwork."

"That's because I finished my paperwork last night. Didn't really have a choice. Seems someone kept me tied up most of the day."

He scratched the back of his neck. "Yeah, about that." Here we go, thought Sophie. He'd come to his senses. "I shouldn't have dropped all my Nate baggage on you like that. The point of the day was for you to relax and let go. Not listen to the long sad tale of my mistakes."

That's what he was apologizing for? Not kissing her, but for sharing a painful memory? True, hearing it altered something inside her; her chest felt incredibly full every time she thought of him trusting her with his tale. But he shouldn't apologize. Ever.

She took the coffee cup he'd helped himself to with a smile. "You told a long, sad tale? I hadn't noticed."

The tease was enough for him to get the message, and he smiled back. "Thanks."

"For what?" She continued to play clueless.

"Just thanks." He touched her shoulder ever so lightly, and Sophie felt the roller coaster cranking anew.

To cover, she reached for the coffeemaker. "Bold, right?"

"Bold and black. By the way, I brought my tape measure." With the apology out of the way, his voice sounded lighter. More like the Grant she'd grown used to. "If you'd like, I can measure for a window."

When she realized what he was offering, she felt a ridiculous shiver of pleasure. The roller coaster ratcheted up another hill. "Does that mean I pass muster?"

His eyes raked her up and down with an approving glint. "You're getting there."

And down went her insides. Tumbling end over end. Forget the roller coaster. She was on one of those free-falling rides where they drop you from the sky.

"Do you miss it?" she asked a little while later. She was perched on her countertop drinking coffee and doing her best to stay out of Grant's way.

"Miss what?" Grant asked in a muffled voice. He lay on his back, head in a lower cabinet.

"Architecture. Being an architect." It was a nosy, pushy question, but after spending the better part of ten minutes trying not to stare at Grant's washboard stomach, she figured nosy and pushy weren't so horrible. "Do you ever regret quitting?"

She got her answer when his screwdriver froze in the air. "No," he replied flatly.

"Not even a little?"

"Sometimes," he corrected with a sigh. "When a client shows me a plan that I know I could do better or if a project doesn't require anything more creative than changing doorknobs and installing light fixtures."

"Like my kitchen," she teased. She thought of the drawings she'd spied on his drafting table. A simple window must not be much of a challenge.

"Your kitchen's different—it comes with coffee. Along with other benefits," he added.

Sophie was grateful his head was in the cabinet so he couldn't see her reaction.

"Doesn't matter," he continued. "I can't go back."

Can't? Sounded awfully final. Grant pushed himself out and sat up. "After Nate's heart attack, I swore to myself I would never be the kind of man I'd become again. I intend to keep that promise."

Through avoidance? Sure sounded that way. "I can understand wanting to bury the past," she began. Heck, she believed wholeheartedly in the practice.

But Grant shook his head. "I'm not burying anything. I'm honoring the past."

Really? Didn't seem that way to her. Sounded more like avoiding, but who was she to judge? She'd been "honoring" for twenty-two years.

Grant changed the subject. "Your hinge is fixed. Should hold you till you decide how much work you want to do in the kitchen."

"I already know how much. I believe you've got the drawings."

"Those were me fooling around. They aren't real designs."

They looked pretty real to her. "You captured

exactly what I was describing. Right down to the color of wood I wanted. Those designs are perfect."

"I told you, they aren't real designs. They aren't even to scale."

"But they could be, right?" she asked him. "I know you said you didn't want to go back to architecture, but one set of plans wouldn't be going back, would it?"

"Was that why you wanted to know if I missed it?"

"No, I was honestly interested." Though now that the subject had come up, she wasn't above taking advantage of the situation. "You've already offered to put in the window. Why not take the project all the way? This could be your chance to finally redo Etta's kitchen. What do you say?"

Grant rolled his eyes, but not before she caught a flash in their depths. His passion wasn't completely extinguished. He wouldn't have started fooling around with those drawings in the first place if it was.

"We'll see," he said finally.

His favorite phrase again. Still, "we'll see" was better than no. In fact, she was pretty sure "we'll see" was closer to yes.

Scrambling to his feet, Grant joined her at the counter, naturally choosing to stand as close as possible. He had his elbow propped on the countertop edge. Sophie could feel the joint abutting her leg. Heat pulsed right through her clothes to her skin.

"You want to see the secret passage?" Grant asked.

Did she! Anything to break the contact. "Sure." She hopped down and headed toward the pantry. It wasn't until she reached up to turn on the light that she realized her error. Her "pantry" was little more than a narrow closet with shelves lined with boxes and canned goods. Grant took up most of the space standing by himself. Adding a second person turned the quarters intimate.

"Here I thought the fridge was well-stocked," he remarked, making his way around her. "You put most supermarkets to shame." Every item had been lined up in a row, with the labels pointing outward. That way, she could find what she needed or didn't need quickly.

"Doesn't that joke get old?" she asked him.

"Hasn't yet." He pushed a stack of cans aside. "Look right here," he said, urging her to move closer. "If you pay close attention, the walls are made of different materials. The side walls are made of horsehair plaster, consistent with materials used in the 1850s. The back wall, however, is drywall, which wasn't used until the twentieth-century. What's more..." He rapped first on the side wall, then on the back. The acoustics were different. "Hollow. That's because there's stairs back there."

"So once upon a time someone would bring the food up from downstairs into my kitchen so it could be served."

"And then bring the dirty dishes back down so the lady of the house never had to see them."

"I could use a service like that myself," Sophie mused.

"My offer still stands."

"I meant having someone whisking the dishes

away. Your offer had more to do with the bedroom and tucking me in."

"Now who's the one turning the conversation into something sexual?"

The question was whispered in the dimly lit, tight quarters, and it was hard not to melt right into him. A very bad idea, Sophie decided. A better idea would be to stack the cans Grant disrupted. She could feel his eyes on her as she meticulously straightened each row, going so far as to make sure the labels of the soup cans faced outward. "You want a level?" he quipped.

"There's nothing wrong with being neat and organized. This way I know exactly what I have and won't be caught—"

"Unprepared." He did his part and straightened a box of pasta. "I bet you were one of those kids who kept all their crayons in nice neat rows and got mad if anyone colored out of the lines."

"Let me guess, you weren't?"

"Oh, no, I always kept my pens and drawing materials nice and neat. In fact, I won 'neatest desk' champion five years running. Would have been six but Jimmy Pierson sabotaged me. My locker on the other hand." He leaned back against the shelves, disrupting another set of cans in the process.

"My mother would forget to buy groceries," Sophie explained, straightening the cans around him. Whether because she felt a kinship with him following his confession or the words simply popped out, Sophie couldn't say. What she did know was that once out, the confession hung in the narrow space.

"She *forgot* to feed you?" Grant asked.

"Not all the time. Just once in a while."

Stiffly, she walked to the sink. His wide-eyed incredulity made her wish she'd never said anything in the first place. Personal issues were best kept quiet and internal.

Grant watched the woman rinsing out their empty coffee cups, shocked at what he heard. No wonder she stocked her pantry like a grocery store. She was afraid of running out of food. The notion confounded him. As busy as his parents were with their careers, he never went without food or warmth or any basics. What else had she gone without? The question broke his heart.

"Where did you grow up?" he asked her. "Was it around here?" He wanted to know more. Everything.

"Upstate New York. Nowhere that matters."

Again, she'd stiffened. Embarrassed. *Don't be,* he wanted to tell her. *It doesn't matter where you came from. Not to me.* "Your family still there?"

She shook her head. "My parents died a few years back and last I knew my brother was living in Ossining."

There was only one place in Ossining that Grant knew of and that was the prison. And, the catch in Sophie's voice when she answered was enough for him to believe that's where her brother was.

She'd obviously had to overcome a lot. Realizing so, the strangest sensation took hold of his chest. It felt fuller than full, like someone pumped his heart full of air. The desire to kiss her, to hold her close and pepper her face with kisses overwhelmed him. He had the sudden urge to tell her the past wouldn't hurt her anymore.

That he would make sure her past demons never touched her again.

Since he couldn't, he settled for tracing his thumb down her cheek. "Impressive," he said.

"Hardly" was her response.

Oh, but it was. She'd shown him a glimpse of herself he knew she didn't show others. A side she kept covered with master plans and designer clothes.

Suddenly it hit him. Who she reminded him of.

When he was a kid, his sister, Nicole, had a blonde china doll with curly hair and a frilly blue dress. It sat on her bed. Few but his family knew that underneath the frills lay a scrollwork of black lines, courtesy of a Magic Marker and a toddler-size Grant.

Sophie was a real-life version of the doll. Beneath the gloss and polish, there existed lines, and she had just shown him a glimpse. Knowing so made his chest grow even fuller. He wasn't going to let this moment slide. "Are you doing anything today besides grocery shopping?" he asked her.

"Work, obviously. Why?"

From the glaze in her eyes, he could tell she was confused. Grant wasn't sure he had a true grasp on what he was about to suggest himself. He only knew he wanted to offer.

"I was wondering," he said, brushing her cheek, "if you'd like to meet Nate."

They drove to a long-term care facility in Long Island. A beautiful stately location with a big lawn and tall pine trees.

"Nate lives here?" When Grant first issued his invitation, she assumed they were going to visit him at his apartment. "I thought you said he had a heart attack?"

"He did. A massive one."

"Then why are we…?"

"By the time they got his heart started again, too much time had gone by."

Her stomach got a sick feeling. "He had brain damage."

"The correct term is 'persistent vegetative state.'"

"I'm so sorry." She seemed to say that a lot,

but what else could she say? She was sorry, for both of them.

A television was playing in Nate's room when they arrived. A baseball game. "Nate's a big Boston fan," he told her, "but since he can't get those games, we make him watch the New York teams. Serves him right for being a traitor."

Sophie studied the man propped in the bed. He was Grant's age and had jet-black hair. Once upon a time, he'd been handsome. Maybe not in Grant's league, but good looking enough to turn heads. The drugs and hospitalization had taken their toll, though, and his face was thin and slack jawed. Blue eyes, which must have been piercing in their day, stared dully into space.

"Hey, buddy," Grant greeted. "I brought some-one to meet you. Remember Sophie? The woman I told you about?"

Sophie was surprised. "You talked about me?" Hopefully he said good things.

"Nate and I talk about everything. Well, I talk and he listens which makes the conversation very Templeton-oriented. He loves that, don't you, pal?"

Sophie stood at the side of the bed, watching Grant interact with his friend. His monologue was overflowing with enthusiasm, an energy-level that had to be draining to maintain. You could tell the chatter was routine, too. There was a natural rhythm to it that told her what she was witnessing wasn't a performance. If Nate did comprehend, he had to be touched by the effort. She was. As she watched, her eyes grew moist.

"I told Sophie all about you, too," he was saying, as he adjusted the bedsheet, "and we figured it was time she got to meet your ugly face."

"Don't listen to him, Nate." Taking a cue from Grant, she moved closer to the bed. "He's just jealous. And don't worry, everything Grant told me was good."

"Most of it anyhow," Grant chimed in. From across the bed, he looked at Sophie and smiled a sad smile.

They stayed for well over an hour. Grant was drained. Visits with Nate always tapped him out, and this visit hit him harder than usual. Watching Sophie from the other side of Nate's bed, it struck him hard that what happened to Nate could have happened to any one of them. Perhaps not an overdose; that blanket of blame still lay at Grant's feet as far as he was concerned. But the determination to get ahead? That was the same.

Sophie had been amazing. Smiling and chatting with Nate as though he were actually responding. Did she, too, recognize the similarities? Or had she gone the extra mile for him? The thought, which had nagged the back of his brain since leaving the nursing home, squeezed at his chest and cut his breath short. It was an uncomfortable feeling, strange and exhilarating. He'd never experienced anything like it before. On top of the fatigue, it left Grant feeling raw and unsettled.

"Should have known you'd take a detour," Sophie remarked.

Distracted, Grant missed his turn. "Sorry," he replied. "Seeing Nate leaves me a little burned-out."

"Do you see him often?"

"Every week. I made a promise I'd keep him a priority."

He felt her hand brush his knee. "You're a good friend."

Oh, yeah, he was a real peach. "There's a diner up ahead," he said, spotting the sign. "Want to stop?"

"Um…I don't know. It's getting late and…"

Man, she was thinking of her freaking to-do list, wasn't she? "Never mind. I forgot you had work to do." The very idea she was thinking about work irritated him. Seeing Nate hadn't shifted a damn thing in her head. He thought… He didn't know what he thought. Angrily, he slapped at the stick shift, turning on his right directional.

"I know what you're thinking," Sophie said, watching him, "and it's not the same. My work ethic and Nate. The situations aren't the same."

"Never said they were," he replied.

"You're thinking it, though. You're not very subtle."

She sat stiff and straight as she stared out the windshield, her gaze focused on someplace far off. "I'm not looking to be number one. I'm just looking to move up as far as I can go. As far away from…"

"What?" Grant wanted to know. He had a pretty decent idea. The empty pantry. The brother in prison. She wanted to get away from the bad memories.

Sophie swiveled in her seat so she could face him. "I'm not like you, Grant. I didn't have an Ivy League education. I've had to work damn hard for everything I've got. Hell, most of the time people expected me to fail. My own family expected me to fail."

"At least you had nowhere to go but up." Her defense only irritated him more. Life on the other side of the fence wasn't all that easy, either. "Try living with success being the only option. In my house, it wasn't good enough to simply be a Boy Scout. You had to be the best damn Boy Scout in the troop, and earn more merit badges than anyone. The Templeton way. Number one or bust." He glanced over, not surprised when he saw Sophie's wide-eyed expression. "You think that sounds better?"

Didn't matter what she thought; he already knew. Knew what lengths the "Templeton way" had led him to. "Things were hard for you, but at least you can look yourself in the mirror with pride for all you've achieved. Maybe if I'd been on your side of the fence, Nate wouldn't be in that hospital bed."

"You don't know that."

"Don't I?"

"No, you don't," she told him. "What happened to Nate wasn't your fault."

"God, I wish people would stop saying it wasn't my fault!" The guilt and all his other feelings reached their tipping point. Yanking the wheel to the right, he steered the truck off the road and slammed to a stop. "Don't you get it?" he asked her. Practically *yelled* at her. "I ignored his phone calls. Five minutes. Five lousy minutes and I couldn't be bothered. I was too busy backstabbing him and scamming old ladies out of buildings to notice my best friend was killing himself!"

His words echoed in the truck, mocking him. He remembered it all clear as day. Nate's mother's anguished expression when she'd told him. His own reflection in the emergency room window. A man in a designer suit he barely recognized. *I don't know who you are,* Nate had screamed at him that afternoon. *Who are you?* The emotions, locked up for the past twenty-eight months finally boiled over, and all the anger and self-loathing he kept buried inside poured out as he smacked the steering wheel over and over. If only he'd tried. If only he'd taken the phone call.

"Stop it," Sophie ordered. She grabbed his arm before he could slap the steering wheel again, fighting with him to hold it back. "Stop beating yourself up. You didn't make Nate take those drugs!"

"I didn't stop him, either."

"No, you didn't. But were you the only person there? What about his family? Your coworkers? Was his well-being your sole responsibility?

"Yes!" In his guilt, the word came out as a shout. "Yes," he repeated, softer. "I knew something was off. I *knew.* That makes it my responsibility."

"If that's true, then am I responsible because my brother dealt drugs?"

"What?" Grant didn't know what she was talking about.

Sophie's eyes glistened with moisture of unwanted memories. "When I was in high school my brother got arrested for dealing pot. I'd known he was up to something for months but never told my family. So was it my fault he became a career criminal to pay for his own habit? Is it my fault my parents couldn't stop drinking or smoking pot?"

"No, of course not. They were addicts." Despite his self-loathing, his chest squeezed. "They wouldn't have listened to you."

"But Nate would have listened to *you*?"

"It's not the same." Grant washed a hand over his face. He appreciated the effort, he really did. All the consolation in the world wouldn't quiet his guilt. Nate's addiction wasn't the real demon here. The demon was the man that Grant feared still existed, waiting for a moment when he could return. "I hate that man," he said, not caring if Sophie understood who he meant or not. He understood. "I hate who he was. A backstabbing, tunnel-visioned…"

Sophie pressed her lips to his, cutting short the rant. She didn't know why she chose kissing to quiet him. She only knew she couldn't stand the self-recrimination any longer. Twice now she listened to him beat himself up. Twice she heard him describe a man that far as she could tell, didn't exist anymore. And so, she shut him up the first way that came to mind. With her kiss, she told him she understood. Understood the need to bury the past. To be so loathing of the past you wanted to keep it and the memories from ever returning. Her kiss was to tell him he wasn't alone. That she was right here with him.

What she miscalculated was the fire that would ignite when they touched. It took less than a second for Grant to kiss her back, and then all coherent thought left her brain. It wasn't long before she found herself sprawled across his lap as she made small mewling noises deep in her throat. She'd never been kissed like this in her life. Not by David, not by anyone. And while she knew it went against everything she'd resolved, she wanted more.

Much to her satisfaction, when the kiss ended, Grant looked as shell-shocked as she felt. Sophie held her breath.

"What was that?" he asked, forehead pressed to hers.

"I don't know." She'd never acted so spontaneously in her life. Words failed her.

Grant's fingers inched their way into her hair, tangling in the strands that worked loose from her ponytail. His breath was hot and minty against her lips. "Let's go home," he wished.

As she seemed to always do where Grant was concerned, Sophie allowed him to lead her away.

CHAPTER NINE

GRANT'S tub was nothing short of amazing. And perfectly sized for two. Sophie knew because she took a nice long soak at Grant's insistence. This time, when she stretched out and felt his breath against her ear, it was because his face was nestled in the crook of her neck. She had to admit, lying there in his arms, she'd never had a better bathing experience.

Later, though, as she dried off and slipped into Grant's blue terry cloth robe, the spell that had begun weaving in the truck had begun to shimmer unstably. What was she doing? The guy was twenty-nine years old. He'd been in elementary school when she started college for crying out loud.

Grant was sitting on the sofa in nothing more than sweatpants when she padded into the room. The minute she saw him, desire stirred again. *I am a dirty old woman,* she thought to herself.

He had been reading something on his phone. Soon as he saw her, he set the phone down. "Feeling relaxed?" he asked her.

"Shouldn't I be asking you that question?" He was the one who had needed comforting, before things turned intimate.

"I feel terrific." He patted the sofa next to her. "Come sit down and stop thinking so hard. I can hear your thoughts."

She wasn't surprised. They sounded pretty loud in her head. "It's just that I never…"

"Shh." He brushed her cheek with her thumb. "I know."

It was so easy to forget her doubts and mistakes when she looked into those eyes. Tucking her legs beneath her, she curled up against him, reveling in the warmth of his bare skin. "Isn't checking emails my job?" she teased.

"It's from a guy I met with a couple weeks ago. He keeps trying to schedule a second meeting even though I already passed on the job. Guy's persistent, I'll give you that."

"What was the job?"

Grant shrugged. "Renovating a high-rise.

Turning the place into modern luxury apartments. He wanted me to head up the project."

"And you turned it down? It sounds like an amazing opportunity."

"I didn't like the design he had in mind. It went completely against the original intent."

Wow, he was the purist, wasn't he? She wondered if he turned down a lot of jobs for that reason.

Or was the reason simply an excuse? After today's meltdown, she wondered if he were simply punishing himself.

"So you're not going to meet with him?"

"I told you, I'm not interested in the job. Besides, I've already promised to do your kitchen."

Had he? She rememberd his answer being a little more noncommittal.

"My kitchen could wait."

"Nothing about you can wait. Although—" he glanced down at his phone screen "—if the guy doesn't stop calling, I'm going to have to meet with him just to make him go away. Obviously, he figures since he's a multimillionaire he can have whatever he wants."

"Must be nice," Sophie murmured, getting up from the sofa.

"Getting whatever you want?"

That, and turning down jobs out of principle. They were both such foreign concepts to her. "All I've ever known was hard work." Climbing up the ladder rung by rung until you got to the top.

Sophie stared out Grant's front windows. Outside, the sky had gone dark, leaving the light to the buildings and the stars. In the distance, she could see the gold dome of the bank building towering over the rest of the borough. "I should probably go downstairs and check my own emails," she remarked. She hadn't looked all day. There were probably dozens of messages from Allen alone.

A pair of warm, strong arms found their way around her waist. "Don't," Grant whispered in her ear. "Stay." Two simple words and they managed to freeze her on the spot.

"Why?"

"Because I like your company. And because you want to."

Sophie smiled. "Says you. Are we going to really repeat this argument?"

"No." In Grant's robe that smelled of peppermint soap and with the warmth of his chest pressed against her, it was difficult to argue the point.

Grant rested his chin on her shoulder. "Was your brother really a dealer in high school?"

"'Fraid so." Another Pond Street family secret. Grant was the first person she'd ever admitted it to. "First of many offenses. I've lost track. My family wasn't exactly Norman Rockwell material."

"You turned out all right."

"Only because I busted my behind to make sure I did."

Peppermint drifted in her direction as he planted a kiss on her neck. "I like that you're showing me the lines," he murmured.

"Lines? I don't understand."

"The stuff underneath all the polish and gloss. I like it."

Now she knew he wasn't making sense. The Sophie she showed him was nothing more than white trash who'd got a scholarship to the local college. She'd done everything in her power to eliminate that person in favor of a better, more sophisticated model. A pearl.

Still, wrapped in his arms, it was nice to pretend for a little while that the old Sophie wasn't so bad.

She returned her attention to the view. Funny, but she always felt small with regards to the world. An insignificant speck dressed up larger than she was, hoping no one found her out. Tonight, however, looking out at Brooklyn, with Grant's arms wrapped around her, she felt bigger. More significant than she'd felt in a long time.

"When I was a little girl, I used to wish I could fly. I'd imagine soaring out my bedroom window and flying all above our town. Everyone would look up and say 'Hey, there's Sophie Messina, the girl who can fly.' I imagine this is what the view would have looked like."

She let her head fall back against his shoulder. "I never told anyone that story before."

Grant smoothed the hair from her face. "What made you choose flying?"

"I was a little girl. I wanted to be special. I wanted—" She didn't finish. She'd wanted to fly away from her life. It'd been the beginning of her master plan. The promise to herself that she would become someone different, live a life as different from her family's as possible. A perfect life with no fights, no crazy drama, no one gossiping behind her back.

A life she controlled.

She didn't say any of it, however. She couldn't because Grant's hands had begun gliding down her shoulders and arms, causing her breathing to catch. His lips delivered butterfly kisses along her temple, her cheekbone. "I know another way to make you feel like you're flying," he murmured as his fingers skimmed her rib cage.

She bet he could. She bet he could take her to heights she never knew possible. Taking hold of his hand, she wrapped her fingers in his. "Show me," she whispered back.

He gladly obliged.

Later that night, Grant stood in front of the window by himself, reliving the weekend. Not at all what he expected when he woke Saturday morning. But then he hadn't expected Sophie, had he?

Sophie. He smiled, his insides warming from thinking her name. She'd surprised the hell out of him this afternoon. Once you scraped off the designer clothes and "I'm a professional" attitude you found a whole cache load of unexpected surprises. Good ones and sad ones. Pretty impressive how she pulled herself out of what sounded like a hellish childhood. Her work ethic started to make more sense.

Wonder if she'd ever stop?

The question disturbed him as much as always. Maybe more. Where did someone like him fit into her master plan, he wondered. Did he even? And if so, for how long?

A noise from behind saved him from his thoughts. Turning, he found the object of his questions in the hallway door. In her hand she held her BlackBerry, obviously purloined from her bag.

"What are you doing?"

"European markets," she answered. Checking the opening numbers.

Grant strolled toward her. She wore his gray T-shirt and her hair was loose and curly. The lips he found so enticing were red and ripe against her pale face. Desire stirred fresh at the sight.

"The numbers can wait," he said, reaching for the phone.

"But…" Though she started to complain, she didn't put up much of a fight; the phone slipped easily from her fingers.

"Later." Dropping the phone to the ground, he wrapped his other arm tightly around her waist and drew her close, until they stood chest to toe.

"Later," she repeated.

Good, they were on the same page. Lowering his lips to hers, he walked her backward to the master bedroom.

Anderson St. Pierre was a pest. No matter how many times Grant said no, the guy wouldn't give up. So here he was, up at dawn to meet him for a breakfast meeting. He'd much rather be in bed with Sophie, trying to coax her into not spending the wee hours of the morning checking the Asian stock market the way she had most of the week.

St. Pierre was already in the diner having breakfast when Grant arrived. "One of the things I love about New York City," he said as Grant took a seat, "is how you can get whatever you want any time of the day. You want fried chicken at the crack of dawn, you got it." He took a bite of a deep fried wing. "You want some?"

"Coffee's fine."

"Suit yourself. This chicken's amazing, though." His host waved a hand and a waitress dutifully hustled over to fill Grant's cup. Ten to one the drink didn't taste nearly as good as the stuff he drank in Sophie's kitchen.

"I'm glad you finally agreed to hear me out," St. Pierre continued.

"Hard to say no when someone calls a half-dozen times. Though I've got to be honest I don't see the point. I already told you I wasn't interested in the job last week."

"Renovating my building. I know." St. Pierre pointed a crinkle fry in his direction. "But what if I doubled your labor costs?"

"What?" Grant choked on his coffee.

"All right, tripled."

The guy was kidding, right? Triple his labor was a boatload of money. "Why?" The offer made zero sense, even if this guy was a billionaire. "There are plenty of contractors around who can do a perfectly good job."

"But none as good as you. I did my research, Templeton. You're good. More than good, and honest, I like to hire the best."

Grant had to chuckle. The man's brazenness rivaled his. "I'm good," he agreed, "at *historical* renovation. Accent on *historical.* What you want to do anybody can do. In fact, I'll even give you some names."

"I want you."

"Yeah, well, if you hire me, I'm going to turn around and ask them to declare your building a historic landmark."

"You should. That building is an original Feldman."

Stunned, Grant stared at the man. "I thought you wanted to gut the place."

"Nah. I just wanted to see how you'd answer." He bit off a bite of chicken. "When you turned me down, I knew I found my man. See, lots of

contractors say they do historical renovations—
I wanted a man who shared my level of vision.
Someone who understood design as well as construction. An award winner."

At the last phrase Grant's blood chilled slightly.
He had done his research. "That was a few years
ago. I'm not with Kimeout anymore. I'm not even
in architecture."

"I know. You're your own man. Exactly what
I want."

"So," Grant said, still trying to figure out what
was going on, "all this talk about tripling my
labor costs was a test?"

"One you passed with flying colors." Pushing
his plate aside, St. Pierre rested his elbows on the
table and leaned forward. "Now, how about we
discuss a real business proposition."

"That has to be the most unorthodox way of
doing business I've ever heard of," Mike said
when Grant called him. His first call had been
to Sophie, but the call had gone straight to voice
mail so he'd turned, reluctantly, to his older
brother.

"I know. And get this, he's developing a housing complex out of an old block of row houses. He wants someone to head the project who has the same mind-set as he does. The person would be in charge of everything from the ground up. Design, construction, personnel. We spent the past two hours talking about the project."

"I owe you an apology, little brother. Turns out being a pain in the butt actually paid off. When do you start?"

"I haven't said yes yet," Grant said, smiling at the waitress topping up his coffee. St. Pierre had provided such an extravagant tip when he left, Grant imagined she'd be happy to pour him coffee all day long if he wanted.

On the other end of the line, he heard silence. Mike, busy rolling his eyes, no doubt. "Why not?" he asked finally.

"For one thing, the job's in Philadelphia."

"So?"

"So, my apartment's here." His life was here. The people he cared about. Mike. Nate.

Sophie. Her name gave him a heavy feeling in his stomach. What would she say about his job offer? She'd probably understand. In fact, she'd understand all too well.

"Philly's not far away," Mike reminded him. "You can drive back and forth in a couple hours. Come back on weekends."

"True, but…"

"But what? What's got you dragging your feet this time?"

Grant didn't know. Yes, he did. They were talking opportunity of a lifetime. Working with Anderson St. Pierre would bring a lot of notoriety. National notoriety. Success. The kind not even Young Architect of the Year could buy. His pulse kicked up a notch, and not in a good way. Would the man—the face from the hospital window—would he return?

"What about Nate?" he asked his brother. The question just came out.

"You come home weekends. Do your penance then."

"My visits aren't penance. Besides his mother, I'm the only visitor Nate has." For how long would he keep the visits going before work and his schedule became an excuse to stay away?

His thoughts returned, unbidden, to Sophie. What about her? Would moving away mean the end of what they began this week? He'd managed to distract her this week, but if he were gone, what then? Would she become so busy she no longer had time for him? How long before their affair fizzled out?

Dread washed over him. He didn't want that to happen. He wanted Sophie. Not for a few days or a few weeks. The realization scared the hell out of him. When did he start thinking of any woman in terms of a relationship? But with Sophie he did. He wanted this thing they had going on for as long as it lasted, maybe even forever.

He needed to see her. Right now. Needed to talk with her and see the reaction in her eyes when he shared his news. To know if this feeling that kept filling his chest was returned.

He needed her.

"I've got to go, Mike." Tossing a second tip on the table, he took off for Wall Street.

CHAPTER TEN

SOPHIE was having a long, lousy Thursday. It began when she slept through her alarm. A week of Grant coaxing her back beneath the covers had started a new habit, which to be honest she enjoyed. A lot.

Unfortunately, her new habit resulted in Allen calling to bark at her. Had she seen the European numbers? Why wasn't she at the office correcting the morning status report? He needed to see her *right away.*

Naturally, his call led to her calling both junior analysts, only to discover they were already in the office. In fact, everyone was in the office already except for her. That mistake she was certain Allen was waiting for her to make? Today was it.

She showered and dressed on the fly, opting to do her makeup during her commute—a decision that even on the best days, didn't turn out well—and arrived at the office a little before eight-thirty, coffee-deprived and underprepared. The only saving grace was the fact that Grant left early for a meeting because if he had been around, then she, in her mad dash to get ready, would have bitten his head off. If Carla, one of her junior assistants, didn't stop smirking at her still-damp hair, she might still bite someone's head off.

"Have you finished revising those figures Allen needed?" she asked, delivering a silent warning to the young woman from over the rims of her reading glasses.

"Put them on your desk fifteen minutes ago," Carla replied.

Sophie thanked her, feeling foolish. She hadn't been this off her game ever. Earlier she even sent an email to Allen and forgot to include the attachment. Her coveted managing director's job felt as if it was slipping from her fingers.

This is karma for having too good a week. You know that, right? She did have a terrific week. Best she could remember in a long time. Best nights, that is, she thought with a smile. Work had been tedious at best. She'd spent the past five days waiting for them to end so she could return to Grant's arms. Scary how much she enjoyed his company. How much she wanted it. Surely the hold he had on her wasn't healthy. Theirs was, at best, a short-term relationship.

Their relationship certainly wasn't healthy for her career right now. Ignoring work for five days had her playing serious catch-up.

"Allen called," Carla piped up over her cubicle wall. "He's looking for the report on Harrington Pharmaceuticals."

"I'll email him a copy right now." Why hadn't Allen called her directly?

Her BlackBerry blinked, indicating a missed call. Allen, she told herself. He must have called when she walked out to Carla's desk. Of course he could have called her office. She was still his go-to person, right? She hadn't lost that title while enjoying the week, had she?

There wasn't time to dwell on the question. The market was going haywire. Up one minute, down three hundred points the next. Clients were bombarding the brokers with questions. Should they sell? Should they buy? It had the entire analysis department scrambling to provide answers.

When noontime rolled around, Sophie didn't notice. She barely had time to breathe let alone eat or grab a cup of coffee. She'd kill for some caffeine!

David called at twelve-thirty. Soon as she heard his bland, unflappable greeting, she got sick to her stomach. She'd been having such a wonderful week, she'd forgotten all about him.

"Thought I'd check the office temperature," he said. "I caught the market scroll on one of the terminal televisions. How are things?"

"Exactly what you'd expect. Wish I had time to clone myself so one of me could run to the bathroom."

"Except you don't know how to harvest DNA."

"I was making a joke."

"I know," he replied, then paused. "Everything all right? Your voice sounds off."

Because she *was* off. "Crazy day is all."

"I understand."

Naturally he did, she thought guiltily. Until she

had a chance to talk to David about Grant, she supposed she was stuck with the stabbing sensation in her stomach. She wished she could tell him now, but after so much time together, she owed the man better.

As it stood, having the conversation face-to-face wouldn't be much easier. What was she supposed to say? *I know we've had an arrangement, David, but it seems I've developed an unhealthy obsession regarding my neighbor.* Wouldn't that go over well. All her plans would go flying out the window.

On the other hand, she couldn't very well keep David in the dark while she waited for this thing she had for Grant to burn out.

No, she was going to have to let David know she was seeing Grant.

Seeing Grant. Such a bland term to describe the week. Was there a word that did? She'd spent the past five days simultaneously excited and scared. Reluctant yet unable to control her behavior. The minute he entered her orbit, her brain ceased working. She felt breathy, giddy. Girlish. Nothing at all like herself.

On his phone at the airport, David seemingly failed to notice she'd drifted off and continued talking in her ear. "With luck," he was saying, "the market will have rebounded by Saturday so we can enjoy a nice quiet dinner. I was hoping to try Troika. I read a review of the place on the plane. Sounds fabulous."

"Sounds good." Wonder if Troika had secluded tables reserved for awkward conversation. She swiped away a few errant strands of hair that had worked their way out of her ponytail. The two of them really needed to talk.

But like everything else today, that would have to wait. No sooner did she hang up with David then she received a call from one of the brokers on the buy side of the company looking for information on health care market projections. A snippy new hire who mistook bossiness for authority, he demanded Sophie have the figures he needed as soon as possible. "Dial it down a notch, Bud," she wanted to say. Moments like this made her seriously consider throwing professionalism to the wind. She was tired, and she didn't need the attitude. If the guy wanted people to treat him with respect, he should try acting like he deserved it. Take Grant, for example. He conveyed authority simply walking into a room.

Grant. She groaned. When did all her thoughts start revolving around him? She woke up thinking about him, she went to bed thinking of him. In between, she wondered what he was doing and if he was thinking about her. When did he become the nexus of her universe?

She had a real problem.

"Allen's still looking for the Harrington report," Carla called.

Give the email a chance to be delivered. "Should be in his in-box in a second," she called back. Carla needn't sound so self-satisfied about her new gopher status.

A knock sounded on her door. "For crying out loud, I said I sent the report," she snapped. "No need to scurry in here to double-check."

"Please don't tell me you're comparing me to a rat."

What? Now she was hearing Grant in her head?

* * *

Looking up from her computer screen, her heart stopped. Unless she'd gone completely round the bend, which was possible given her obsession, Grant stood in the doorway.

"Grant?" she asked. Just to make sure.

"I take that as a yes." He strolled in wearing faded jeans and a summer wool blazer. Suave meets sexy. From behind his shoulder Sophie saw the head of every female employee, along with a couple males, peering over their cubicle walls. The man literally caused work to stop. *This is how you command authority.*

"Bad time?" he asked in his slow-honeyed voice. Her body immediately reacted. She definitely had it bad. Very bad.

Clearing her throat, she pulled herself back to reality. "What are you doing here?"

"I, um…" There was uncharacteristic hesitation in his voice, along with an emotion in the back of his eyes she couldn't quite define. "Coffee?" He held a green-and-white cup in her direction.

Talk about reading her mind. "I was just dreaming of a cup."

"Must have been sharing a psychic moment."

Their fingers brushed as he handed her the cup, sending sparks up her arm. He dipped his head slightly and leaned toward her cheek. Sophie felt her body sway, drawn as always by his inexplicable pull. If they weren't in her office…

But they were in her office, and people were watching. Abruptly, she pulled back, leaving him leaning into air. Surprise and something more—hurt?—flashed across his face.

"Thank you. For the coffee." Hoping the heat coming off the cup would burn away the feelings rippling through her body, she curled her fingers tightly around the cup.

"Well, I know how much you appreciate your caffeine."

The air in the office felt thick and awkward. She could see the junior analysts still stealing glances. Sophie's nerves started rising. Tomorrow she'd be topic number one on the office grapevine; if it took that long. She could already see Carla's devious little gleam. Might as well take out an ad in the company newsletter—Senior Analyst Caught Mooning Over Boy Toy.

Grant was watching her, too, with an inscrutable expression that made her insides even more self-conscious. "Was coffee the only reason you came by?" she asked, smoothing her hair. Even if her insides were trembling, she could at least give the appearance of professionalism.

"Do I need more of a reason?"

No. That is, *yes.* That is, "Things are really crazy here at the moment. Unless you have something important…"

Another flash of that emotion. "I did, but I've decided it can wait."

"Are you sure?" She was getting an uneasy feeling about the emotion she saw.

"Sophie, about this Harrington report. Do you have the figures broken down by month?"

Terrific. Exactly the person she didn't want popping in.

"Hello, Allen," she greeted, pretending as though having a stranger in her office was perfectly routine. "I'll pull those figures up right now."

"If it's no problem." His critical stare moved from her to Grant and back. Her already jumpy stomach plummeted. *Hop. Skip. Drop.*

"I was on my way out, anyway," Grant said. "I'll talk to you later."

"Don't rush on my account," Allen said. Naturally he didn't mean a word. Sophie could feel his impatience burning a hole in her profile. Outside, Carla and the others were watching, waiting, too.

"Grant just stopped by to deliver an estimate."

The lie flew out before she could stop herself. Allen looked as though he expected an explanation and delivering an estimate sounded so much more appropriate. Silently, she looked to Grant for help, only to realize too late, the mistake she'd made. The shutters had slammed down over Grant's eyes and what were once warm and expressive stared at her cold and hard.

"Delivering an estimate in person? Don't see that kind of personal service much anymore."

"What can I say," Grant replied with an edge only Sophie would recognize. "I'm very hands-on. And Ms. Messina was a special case."

Was? She didn't think it possible for her stomach to drop further, but it did.

Grant's eyes burned hotter than any stare of

Allen's. "Now that our business is over, I'll get out of your hair. I know how important Ms. Messina considers her work to be."

"Grant..." She wanted to grab his arm, ask him to stay so she could apologize. Explain herself. With Allen standing there, however, she could do little more than offer silent regret. "I'll talk with you tonight," she told him, "so we can sort everything out."

"No rush. I think everything's crystal clear." After offering up a handshake to Allen, he tossed one last crisp nod in her direction and left. Sophie was forced to watch his back as he marched away.

"Now about those figures," Allen said, voice clipped.

"Pulling them up on the screen now." Sophie returned to business. She'd apologize to Grant tonight.

Hopefully, he'd listen.

CHAPTER ELEVEN

THE best laid plans will go wrong. Wasn't that Murphy's Law? If not, Murphy said something awfully close, and Sophie was pretty sure he'd been talking about her day. Management's demands kept her at the office until well after ten.

Getting out of her taxi, she looked to the second floor and found Grant's windows dark. Disappointment washed over her. The past few days, he'd kept them on for her. Then again, she'd come home much earlier. Chances are he was watching his game in the bedroom and simply turned out the front lights to look like he was asleep, but in case he did go to bed early, she'd wait and apologize in the morning. Dragging the man out of bed didn't seem like the best way to mend fences. She'd apologize tomorrow morning when they got together for morning coffee. A good night's sleep and he'd have cooled off, putting him in a better position to accept her apology. After all, surely once he thought things through he'd realize she didn't mean to insult him.

Problem was, he didn't show up. Sophie heard his boots on the stairs, but the steps continued straight out the front door, leaving her with two cups of coffee and a kernel of uneasiness rolling around in the pit of her stomach.

Fine. They'd talk when she got home. Just to be certain, she scribbled a quick note and slipped it under his door.

Grant was seated on the stairs when she arrived home, thirty minutes after the time she wrote on her note. Seeing him, her throat thickened and her chest grew tight. The door clicked thunderously behind her. "Hi." The ache in her chest made the words a whisper. "You got my note."

Grant looked up. Cool brown eyes threatened to bore straight through her, and the longing she felt seconds early turned to unease. "You're late. You said five-thirty."

So much for a good night's sleep helping him

cool off. "Allen dumped a project on us last minute. Took more time than I expected."

"Of course it did."

Doing her best to ignore the sarcasm, she smoothed her skirts and took a seat next to him. His peppermint soap teased her nostrils and it was all she could do not to close her eyes and inhale. Lord, but she'd missed him. She didn't realize how much until she saw him again. Hopefully they could put this incident behind them soon so things could go back to the way they were.

"If you want to talk about your quote, you're going to have to be quick. I've got to get to Long Island."

Sophie flinched. "You're still angry."

"You think?" Up close his eyes were even colder, like winter in August. "You told your boss I was your contractor."

"Well, you are doing my kitchen...."

"Really? Tell me then, what do you call what we've been doing the past few nights? Negotiating?"

"It was a joke."

"I didn't find it very funny."

Obviously. Her dreams of a quick resolution faded away. "Look, I'm sorry I told Allen you were my contractor. It was a mistake."

"No kidding."

But she'd apologized. Surely that should be enough. "It's just that Allen caught me off guard. Both of you did. What were you doing there anyway?"

He shook his head. "Doesn't matter now."

No, she supposed not. "Point is, had I known you were coming by I would have been better prepared. I could have—"

"Come up with a better cover story?"

"Stop putting words in my mouth." He wasn't being fair. "I admit I was wrong, but think about it for a second, Grant. What exactly was I supposed to say?"

"Gee, let me think." He leaned his back against the railing, increasing the distance between them. "I know! How about the truth?"

Which was what? *Hey, Allen, here's the guy I'm sleeping with?* Oh, yeah, that would have worked out really well.

Her thoughts must have played out on her face,

because Grant suddenly sighed and shook his head. "You know, I really thought we were over this age difference thing."

"What are you talking about?"

"You're obviously embarrassed to be seen robbing the cradle."

"Don't be absurd. Just because I don't want the office to know my business doesn't mean I'm embarrassed."

"Really? Sure could have fooled me."

"Why, because I won't shout our affair to the world? Excuse me for wanting to keep my professional life and my private life separate."

"But you're not embarrassed," he muttered under his breath.

Dear God. If her hair wasn't in a ponytail, she'd pull her hair out. Why was he being so difficult? She said she was sorry, for crying out loud. Besides, he should understand the circumstances. "For God's sake, Grant, it's not like we're talking about some random coworker. This was Allen Breckinridge, the most senior managing director. The man literally holds my future in the palm of his hand."

An undecipherable look clouded his eyes. "Allen holds your future," he repeated flatly.

"Yes." They'd discussed this. "He's in charge of naming the new managing directors. I screw up with him, and I've screwed up my career. You know how important becoming managing director is to me."

"Oh, I know. Do me a favor, and remind me not to stand in the way if you're ever in the line for chairman of the board. Instead of throwing me under the bus, you might actually push me in front of one."

"Stop being childish."

"Childish?" He blinked. "*I'm* being childish? No way. I'm not the one too immature to realize there's more to life than a freaking promotion."

"Like what, burying your head in the sand? Excuse me, but not all of us have the luxury of hiding out because we're afraid of the future. Some of us need to keep working to make something of ourselves."

It was a low blow. Grant's eyes narrowed. "What's that supposed to mean?"

"Nothing." She wasn't in the mood to psycho-analyze his guilty conscience right now.

But Grant didn't want to let go. "I'm not burying my head anywhere. You know damn well why I stepped off the fast track, Sophie."

"Yeah, I know why. I also know you've been hell-bent on trying to convince me to jump off with you."

"Excuse me for not wanting you to repeat my mistakes."

"And excuse me for not wanting to throw away twenty years of hard work on a fling!"

She whipped the words at him so hard he visibly flinched. His shoulders dropped slightly, and the look from before, that unreadable, disturbing look, returned to his eyes. "That how you see this? As a fling?"

"How else am I supposed to see 'this'?" she asked, her own voice dropping. "For all I know, we could fizzle out next week."

"Maybe, maybe not. Isn't that part of the risk in a relationship?"

Maybe. "I don't take risks, remember?"

"I know. I've seen your pantry."

"Then you should understand."

"But what if I asked you to?" he asked suddenly, looking her straight in the eyes. "What if I asked you to tell Allen and your entire office that we are together?"

The hairs on the back of her neck stood on edge. Tell Allen? It wasn't that simple. Allen demanded his employees give their whole lives to the job.

She took too long to answer. Grant immediately shoved himself to his feet. "Forget I asked. You've obviously made your choice."

"Grant—" There wasn't a choice to be made. She'd worked too long and too hard to become the Sophie Messina the world knew. To ruin that reputation for a fling...

It was a fling, right? A relationship with no future? Because she hadn't planned on... The hairs on her neck began to rise.

"Where are you going?" she called, seeing Grant heading for the front door.

"To Long Island. Nate's waiting."

"What about our conversation?"

He gave a soft, bitter laugh. "What about it? I

asked you to tell Allen about us and you said no. There isn't much more to say, is there?"

"Except, I didn't say no."

"No, you hesitated. For the second time," he added.

"Because what you're asking is complicated. After I'm promoted I'll be glad to tell people."

He shook his head. "You still don't get it, do you?"

No, she got it. He was the one who didn't understand. How hard she worked. How much she needed this promotion. "Do you have any idea how hard it was for me to get to where I am? The demons I had to outrun?" He wasn't the only one with a past they wanted to erase. "There's a lot more at stake here than just your ego."

Ego? Grant blinked. She thought this was about ego? Grant stared at the woman sitting on the stairs. Took every ounce of self-control not to grab her by the shoulders and shake sense into her. "You're right," he said, his jaw squeezed so tightly it hurt. "There was a lot more at stake." And she blew it.

If he stayed in the foyer another second, he would lose his temper and do something stupid, so he spun on his heel and walked out the door, leaving Sophie sitting on the stairs. Alone. The way she apparently wanted it.

Allen holds my future in the palm of his hand. Allen. Her freaking boss! He wanted to punch something. He settled for punching the steering wheel.

God, but he was such a fool. He slammed the door of his truck so hard the glass rattled. Dammit all! He should have known better. Her past hurts ran too deep. She was too afraid of, he didn't know what, being left without, that she made her choice.

And she called him afraid? Ha!

An emptiness like he hadn't felt in years engulfed him, extinguishing his anger and replacing it with a giant hole. He'd thought she... That they... The emotion danced on the tip of his brain, too hesitant to reveal itself by name.

What did he do now? Go back to Sophie's bed and settle for being second best? Pride wouldn't let him. Then again, the idea of passing by her door every day, of being so close and yet not close enough held even less appeal.

There was, he realized, a third option. Absentmindedly, his fingers curled around his cell phone.

The opportunity of a lifetime.

Nate would want him to.

Sophie wouldn't care.

Afraid, huh? He'd show her afraid. Opening the contacts folder, he scrolled down to *S* and dialed.

On Saturday, Sophie attacked her usual chores. They didn't take nearly as long as usual. Probably because there was no banging to distract her. The building was quiet as a church.

Too quiet.

For what felt like the thousandth time, she replayed last night's conversation with Grant. Her actions back at her office were wrong; she admitted as much. Why then couldn't he accept her apology and move on? What did it matter when or if she told the world they were involved?

Was their relationship that important to him? She thought about the dark expression in his eyes when she referred to what they had going on as a fling. Thinking back, it had looked awful close to hurt or disappointment. An unreadable emotion of her own took flight in her stomach.

No, she thought, calming the flutters. They were just having a fling. A wonderful, intoxicating fling.

Or least they had been. The way Grant walked off last night felt a lot more final than what she wanted. She missed him. Fling or not, she wasn't ready to give him up. Soon as she talked with David she'd head upstairs. See if she couldn't smooth things over.

Spurred on by her plan, she called David and asked if he could come by earlier than scheduled. Sooner they talked, the sooner she could go see Grant. The lawyer's amiable agreement made her conscience cringe. David had been the man she expected to spend her future with. When had her plans gotten so turned around?

An hour later, she heard the front doorbell ring. Immediately her nerves went into overdrive. "Relax," she told herself. David was a reasonable man. He'd understand what happened even if she didn't. After all, wasn't that his best quality? His ability to understand.

David's blue eyes widened when she opened the door. "Shorts?" he asked. "A little casual for Troika, don't you think? Never mind, you look lovely anyway." He leaned in to kiss her hello. Sophie tilted her head so his lips caught her cheek instead. "I missed you while I was in Chicago," he said.

A noise sounded in the entranceway behind them. Anxiety gripped her. Sophie closed her eyes. Grant. His body was stiff, his expression cold. "Don't let me interrupt the reunion."

Sophie's heart sank. She knew what he was thinking. Just knew. Catching his eye, she tried to let him know he was mistaken.

The message was ignored.

"Hello." Oblivious to Sophie and Grant's silent conversation, David extended a hand. "Sophie's neighbor, right? The man with the bathtub. Got it inside I see."

"Yes." Though he shook David's hand, Grant's eyes stayed locked on hers. Narrow slits that burned into her skin. "Everything is right in place. Isn't that so, Sophie?"

"I don't know," she replied. Two could play the cryptic game. "Is it?"

"From my view, anyway." He turned to David. "The two of you on your way out?"

"Yes, we're having dinner at Troika, soon as Sophie changes."

"Troika. Sounds special. I hope you don't have to wait long. For Sophie to change, that is."

"Oh, I don't mind waiting. After all our months together, I'm used to being patient. Isn't that right, Sophie?"

Sophie didn't reply. She wasn't sure who was annoying her more at the moment. Grant with his veiled remarks, or David who had suddenly decided to act possessive and drape his arm around her shoulder. As delicately as possible, she slipped out of his grasp. "We should probably go inside. I'll fix you a drink while you wait."

"Sounds great. You can tell me about your plans for renovating your kitchen. You're going to be doing the work, aren't you?" he asked Grant.

Was he trying to bury her?

"Hopefully you'll be able to talk her into modernizing. Maybe if she hears from a contractor, she'll listen. I've been telling her to gut the whole place and start from scratch, but she keeps dragging her feet."

"Well, you know Sophie. She doesn't do anything without a master plan." The words, delivered with cool cordiality, sliced through her. But then he'd meant them to.

"Yes, she does tend to stick to her plans," David agreed.

"Not necessarily," Sophie replied. She looked at both of them, hoping they each got the intended message. "In fact, I hoped to talk with Grant later this evening about my plans."

"Unfortunately, I won't be able to be part of any plans," Grant replied. "I'm leaving town. I've decided to take a job in Philadelphia."

"You have?" His comment cut her at the knees. Philadelphia? "I didn't know…" She had no clue there was a job to be taken.

"I only recently decided. I'm taking a job with St. Pierre Development."

"Oh." Grant was leaving. Going to Philadelphia.

No more nights wrapped in his arms. No more early morning cajoling to stay under the covers. No more coffee in her homely, cramped kitchen.

She swallowed the lump stuck in her throat. "I didn't think you wanted the job."

"Originally, no, but when we met Thursday morning, he made me an offer that was hard to turn down."

Thursday. Same day he'd showed up at her office. She knew he'd had something on his mind. And she'd chased him off. This was her fault. Her doing.

"Congratulations," she heard David say. "Working for a man like Anderson St. Pierre will open a lot of doors for you careerwise."

"So I'm told. And since there's nothing holding me here…"

Sophie's stomach dropped another notch. "Are you sure there's nothing?"

"Positive." His gaze was harsh and pointed, challenging even. "Unless you know a reason why I should stick around?"

Yes, she wanted to say. *Me. Stick around with me.* But David was standing there, and besides, hadn't she determined they were only having a fling? He was finally moving forward, making plans to do something with his life. Who was she to stop him?

"When do you leave?" It took some effort, but she managed to ask without her voice cracking.

Although the glimmer of pain she caught passing behind his eyes was almost her undoing. "Soon. Anderson wants to start the project as soon as possible."

Meaning this might be the very last time they saw each other. The lump in Sophie's throat spread to her chest, the ache so strong it threatened to choke her.

The trio stood in awkward silence. There were things Sophie wanted to say. Things like "Don't go." But, the words wouldn't come. *Let him go, Sophie. It's over.*

David cleared his throat. "We should let your neighbor get going," he said. "We," as if they were a united force. "I'm sure he has a busy evening."

"As a matter of fact, I do," Grant agreed. He gave her one last look before heading toward the stairs. "Goodbye, Sophie."

"Wait!"

Grant turned around. "Yes?"

Let him go, Sophie. Let him go. "Good luck," she finally managed to choke out. It wasn't what she wanted to say, but it was the best thing to say.

He nodded. "You, too, Sophie."

To his credit, David waited until Grant's apartment door shut before speaking up again. "Philadelphia, huh? Thank goodness. Now maybe you can get over this construction worker fantasy of yours and things can get back to normal."

Whipping her head around, Sophie stared at him. His blue gaze was as dispassionate as ever.

And to think, she'd thought him oblivious. In reality, he was merely indifferent. That calmness and understanding she thought so wonderful was apathy. "Actually, David, I don't think so," she said. "I think you should leave."

He blinked. "But we have reservations at Troika."

Unbelievable. Missing their reservations. That's what finally managed to upset him.

"Sorry," she said, no longer caring about his feelings. Hard to hurt something that barely registered. "I'm too busy nursing my 'construction worker fantasy' to feel like eating. You'll just have to head to Troika by yourself."

She left him standing in the foyer, mouth slightly ajar. It was, perhaps, the most emotional she'd seen him the entire time they'd been together.

Soon as she closed the door, however, her satisfaction drained away and her heart began to ache once more.

Thank goodness for work. It kept her mind occupied all Saturday night and all day Sunday. There was a sort of fitting irony to the situation; the very thing Grant accused her of being obsessed with keeping her from obsessing over Grant. After parting ways with David, she thought of running upstairs and banging on Grant's door, but what purpose would that serve?

How about keeping him in your life?

No. Grant was not part of her life. He had been a momentary detour. A wonderful, unplanned weeklong fling that was now over. It was time to refocus her energies.

Monday morning she took extra care getting ready for work, applying her makeup so her sleeplessness wasn't visible. Her lack of sleep was solely due to staying up late working, not because she was ruminating over Grant. She had a lot of ground to make up after her recent "distraction." To sustain her efforts, she pulled out her favorite power suit, a black sheath dress and red-cropped jacket that made her look sophisticated and intimidating. She dug out her black patent leather stilettos, too. Surveying her reflection, she decided with satisfaction, the world would see a woman who had her act together. Certainly not a woman who was mourning the loss of her upstairs neighbor.

When she strode into her building, she felt a little more on course. She would be fine. Eventually her continuous thoughts about Grant would end. In the meantime, she had a job to do. Rumor had it that senior management had been sealed up in meetings over the weekend to discuss the upcoming changes in leadership. Meaning an announcement could be made any day now.

The floor was buzzing with energy when she

stepped off the elevator. Apparently she wasn't the only one who'd heard the rumors. About ten o'clock, she got a phone call from Allen Breckinridge asking her to join him in the conference room.

"Certainly," she said, her stomach giving an involuntary nervous jump. *Relax, Sophie. He could simply want to talk about last week's figures.* Grabbing hard copies of her reports, she headed upstairs.

She always loved meeting in the conference room. Located on the twelfth floor, the room had large windows that let you look out at the buildings across the street. One in particular had beautiful stonework surrounding the windows. Grant would appreciate the stonework, she thought without thinking. Just as quickly, she pushed it away. Grant wasn't here.

Through the interior windows, she saw Allen and two other members of the Twamley Greenwood management team seated inside. Suddenly her palms began to sweat. She normally wouldn't meet with a group unless something important was afoot. After discreetly wiping her hands on her skirt, she knocked on the door. Allen waved her in. As she entered, the other two heads turned to greet her.

"Come in, Sophie," Allen greeted. "Take a seat."

Palms sweating again, she eased into an empty seat next to Raymond Twamley, the outgoing partner. The senior man nodded in greeting.

"I'll get right to the point," Allen said. "You've been a valuable member of our team for several years now, Sophie. Personally I know I've come to appreciate your contribution and dedication. Your hard work has helped me more than once."

Oh, my God, this was it. She folded her hands and squeezed them tightly. "I've enjoyed working here, Allen," she replied.

"It shows. Which is why we've asked you here this morning. As you know, Raymond is stepping down at the end of the year, leading us to make some managerial changes."

Sophie held her breath. In the back of her mind, Grant's memory threatened to spoil the moment. She shoved him aside.

"After careful discussion," Allen said, "we've

agreed you should replace Raymond as the next managing director."

She exhaled. At last. Twenty-two years of late hours and weekends had finally paid off. The little girl from Pond Street was no more. She was now one of them. A managing director. One more box checked off on her master plan.

She always thought the moment would have more resonance.

"Thank you, Allen," she said with a professional smile. Now was not the time to worry about why she wasn't excited. "Your confidence in me means a lot."

Allen, now her peer, looked at her with cool regard. "Don't let us down."

The moment of equality faded away. "I won't."

"Good. Now, on to business. We need you to fly to Boston tonight..." He continued on, outlining a work schedule that made her current week look like a vacation.

So much for her moment of glory. She told herself she'd celebrate in Boston.

Later that afternoon she swung by her apartment to pack. The office had her booked on a seven o'clock shuttle to Logan Airport. As she walked through the front door, a brown cardboard tube propped by her door caught her eye. Sophie's stomach began to twist. Delivery men didn't just leave packages. Not in New York. Either someone who knew her signed for it or...

Or someone from the building left it for her.

She brought the tube inside and, setting it on her dining room table, reached for the attached note. Her hands shook as she saw the male scrawl on the paper.

It was a list of contractors and phone numbers. Nothing more. No goodbye. No initial. Only a list.

Her euphoria over being promoted faded away. She let the list drop from her fingers, letting it fall to the table.

Suddenly she didn't feel like celebrating anymore.

CHAPTER TWELVE

A MONTH later, Sophie found herself alighting from a taxi, home after another week of back and forth travel to Boston. As she stepped onto the pavement, she sighed and, as she did every night, looked up to Grant's front windows. As they were every night, the windows were dark.

Far as she knew, he'd been home only a few times since leaving. On weekends. Two weeks ago, she'd heard the sound of footsteps on the stairs and pretended to get her mail as an excuse to check. Unfortunately, all she got was a view of his legs turning the corner at the top of the stairs. She'd been about to call to him when she stopped herself. He saw the lights on in her apartment; if he'd wanted to say hello, he would have knocked.

Now she paid the taxi driver, collected her receipt and slowly made her way to the front steps, her overnight bag dragging behind her, *dragging* being the operative word. The past thirty days she had traveled from New York to their Boston office a dozen times. She was bone tired.

At least she was finally home. Leaving her bag in the living room, she padded her way past the panel doors, sorting through the mail as she did. The knowledge failed to thrill her as it normally did. Oh, she still loved her apartment, but the place felt off. Not quite as perfect as it had when she first bought the place at the beginning of the summer. Longing welled up inside of her as she ran a palm across the dining room wood work.

Perhaps if she did something about the kitchen. The designs Grant did for her lay on her dining room table, the list of contractors still where she dropped it a month earlier. She should start calling them, asking for references and quotes. No doubt any of them would do excellent work. After all, Grant had recommended them.

Maybe when she wasn't so tired, she decided, staring at the crack made by the molding joints. Her stomach hurt right now. Nothing serious.

Just a heavy, deadlike feeling that never seemed to go away. Hadn't since…

God, she should be past this by now. She dug her fingers into her hair, pulling the strands so tight the bangs worked loose of the clip holding them. Grant, Grant, Grant. He wouldn't leave her thoughts. Just when she thought she'd banished him from her head, something would make his memory come screeching back. A glimpse of sandy-brown hair. The contents of her coffee cup. The other day, she lost her train of thought during a presentation because one of the women in the conference room had been drinking peppermint tea.

Face it, Sophie. The guy is still under your skin. More than that. He was inside her. He had a far greater hold on her feelings than she cared to admit.

So lost in her rambling thoughts was she, she didn't think about grabbing her cell phone until the black square was in her palm. *You don't even know his cell phone number.* Talk about irony. The man owned her thoughts and she hadn't known him long enough to add him to her contacts. But then she hadn't had to. He was always right upstairs.

Not anymore, though.

Giving another long sigh, she carried her cell phone into the bedroom. If she could call him, what would she say? Miss you? Can't stop thinking about you? Please come back? The guy was finally moving forward, away from the guilt that had been holding him back. She should be focusing on her new job and her own future plans.

Besides, she thought, looking at her tired reflection, as if she had any business being involved with a man like Grant anyway. She was no glamorous cougar. She was still Sophie Messina from Pond Street. Turns out the promotion hadn't chased those demons away after all.

The lines around her mouth deepened as she frowned. Her fingers brushed along their groove, pulling the skin taut and letting it go. No, she repeated. She was no cougar. Just a tired financial executive who'd taken a brief detour from life's well-laid-out road and got momentarily distracted by the view. And right now what this tired financial executive needed was a long hot bath and a good night's sleep so she had the strength to get up and do it all again early tomorrow morning.

You only have to keep up this pace for a few years, she reminded herself when she groaned. *Then you can get that summer house like you wanted and rest there.*

For the first time, focusing on the next goal didn't help. Chasing the next rung didn't seem all that desirable anymore. She'd much rather smell the peppermint.

Next morning she got up, cleaned, paid her bills and found herself with an excess of energy. Without the continual banging from upstairs, her apartment was way too quiet. Too quiet to concentrate. Her knee kept bouncing up and down, and she had trouble focusing on the numbers. Figuring a run might help, she dug out her running shoes. They were in the back of her closet. She hadn't gone running since…

Don't go there. She was going to try and spend one day not dwelling on Grant.

Turned out, endorphins were the perfect tonic. After four weeks of road travel, her body loved being outside, and the late summer day made the run that much more pleasant. She took the path in the park and just kept going.

Before she realized, she'd reached the flea market. The sign on the front gate caused her to draw up short. Last Weekend, it read. A sense of sadness settled on her shoulders, the way it did when a season was ending. Without thinking, she retrieved the emergency money she kept in her shorts pocket, and paid the entrance fee.

The market was as crowded today as it had been her first visit, and if possible, the rows more overwhelming and hard to navigate. Then again, her other visit had been with Grant. If she remembered correctly, she'd been too dazed by him to worry about the crowd. What she wouldn't give to be wandering the booths with him now.

He'd looked so commanding that afternoon. Every inch the capable, confident man he was. She knew men twice his age that would kill for an ounce of Grant's natural abilities. No wonder she'd fallen for him, despite his age. He was a man well beyond his years.

After several meandering turns, she wound her

way to the back row where Grant purchased his lighting fixtures. The old man who they visited wasn't there today. In his place was a pair of young men in their twenties selling what looked like auto parts.

The vintage clothing booth was still in the same place, though. Sophie saw the vendor chatting up a customer near a display of jewelry.

She poked her way through a vintage hat display and looked at a couple of 1980s handbags, then turned right. The rack of coats was in the same place as before, still filled with brightly colored fashions. A big sign read Last Chance, Thirty Percent Off. Curious, Sophie picked through the garments, noting the large number of floral dresses and old fur coats. One garment, however, looked to be missing.

"Can I help you?" The vendor appeared at her shoulder.

"I was here about a month ago with a friend," Sophie said. "He was doing business with an older gentleman in the booth next door."

"Oh, yes, the tall, sandy-haired man." Of

course, she'd remember Grant. "He comes here often."

The woman leaned forward and whispered conspiratorially. "Very nice."

Sophie resisted saying thank you since Grant wasn't hers anymore. "You had a coat I tried on that day. Blue with fur cuffs."

"Blue with fur cuffs. Sounds familiar." The woman thought for a moment. "Brocade right? Fur collar and matching cloth buttons."

"Exactly."

The woman waved her rings in the air. "I sold that piece weeks ago."

"Oh," Sophie replied, disappointed.

"If you'd liked it, though, I've got a cape with a fur collar. Bright red."

"No, thank you. I was only interested in the blue one."

"Sorry. Place like this, when you see something special, you gotta grab it. Otherwise you'll miss out."

Apparently so. Disappointed, Sophie thanked her and headed on her way. It was only a coat, she told herself. No big deal. And yet, in the back of her mind, she couldn't shake the thought she was missing out. It was the same unnerving feeling she'd had the first time. She really wished she knew why an old coat was causing her so much bother.

The crowd seemed bigger on the way out. Sophie swore it had not only doubled in size, but stopped moving, as well. She craned her neck to see what caused the delay, but didn't see anything. Then, out of the corner of her eye, she saw it. A flash of sand-colored hair on her right. A tingle moved down her spine. She wove her way closer to the booth where she'd spotted him. It was an antique furniture dealer a dozen booths down. His back was to her, and his head was bent as he examined a Victorian-era chaise. Didn't seem like Grant's style, but perhaps it was for his new job.

She moved a little closer, excited to surprise him. Maybe she could convince him to grab a bite to eat on the way home. As friends. To make up for all that happened between them. It would be a good first step, and lay the groundwork for later.

Three or four booths closer, she was about to call out his name. Her mouth had barely opened when suddenly a petite brunette sidled up and joined him. Sophie's heart sank as the woman wrapped her arms around his narrow waist. *No.*

The man turned his head, and to Sophie's relief, she didn't recognize the profile. Now that she looked closer, she realized the man's posture was all off, as was his build. He lacked Grant's broad shoulders and natural self-possessed carriage. Actually, the only resemblance at all was the sand-colored hair. Her mind made up the rest.

Slowly her heart rate returned to normal. The clothing vendor's advice came rushing back. *When you see something you like, you got to act fast or miss out.*

CHAPTER THIRTEEN

"PHILADELPHIA treating you well?"

"Good enough. Saw the Liberty Bell."

"What's St. Pierre like to work for?"

"Eccentric. He's the one who dragged me to the Liberty Bell."

"Okay, do you want to talk about it?"

Grant looked up from his plate. "Huh?"

"Whatever's bothering you," Mike asked. "Do you want to talk about it?

"No." He did not want to talk. He did not want to mention Sophie's name. Sophie with her perfect, kissable lips and her age-appropriate companion who had dominated his thoughts for the past month.

"Okay." His brother shrugged and reached for his imported lager, the buttons on his navy blazer reflecting the glow of recess lighting. Only Mike would wear a blazer to a sports bar on a Saturday afternoon. His idea of casual dress.

"Mom and Dad tell you they were going to France?" he asked instead.

"They are?"

"This fall. Apparently the idea's been on Mom's bucket list for years."

Terrific. Another woman with a bucket list. Grant stabbed at the ketchup with his French fry. "What is it with people and bucket lists, anyway?" he asked aloud. "If you want to go to Paris, just go. Why do people have to make a production out of everything by making a list of 'someday items.'" He'd had his fill of goals and life plans.

Mike set down his bottle. "Okay, what's wrong?"

"Nothing's wrong. I don't like bucket lists is all." Especially when checking off the items on the list means more than the people in your life.

"Uh-huh."

"Seriously."

"Then why are you smashing the life out of your French fries?"

Grant looked down at the potato wedge,

smushed and half-drowned in ketchup. Maybe he did need to talk, if for no other reason than to get the woman out of his head. Stewing alone in his hotel room certainly wasn't working.

"If you must know, it's Sophie."

"Who?"

"The downstairs neighbor. My former downstairs neighbor."

"The 'cease and desist' lady."

"Yeah, her." He'd forgotten Mike didn't know the whole sordid story. "Before I left town, we were—" he scratched the back of his head "—seeing each other."

His brother blinked over the rim of his glass. "You were? Last I knew, she'd ticked you off and you reacted very poorly."

"Let's say I repeated the pattern." Starting from the beginning, he laid out what happened, ending with the scene in Sophie's office. "So I broke things off and took the job with St. Pierre."

"Ouch." Mike swallowed his beer. "Relegated to dirty little secret. I can see how that hurt."

More than Grant thought possible. It felt as if someone sucked the heart out of his chest and stomped on it. Then stomped on it again when she called their relationship a fling and said Allen was the key to her future. He'd thought by now the ache would have subsided, but the more time passed the worse he felt. He missed her like crazy. Her and her maddening behavior.

"I can see her point, though," Mike added.

Grant stabbed another fry into the ketchup. "Why am I not surprised?"

"Hey, I didn't say I agreed with how she treated you. But there are companies out there that demand one hundred and ten percent. Personal lives come second. If her career is that important to her…"

"It's everything to her."

Tired of destroying his food, Grant sat back in his chair. Thing is, he hadn't asked her to give up her career. He'd simply wanted to be on equal footing with her career aspirations. More than anything, he wanted to know their relationship meant something to her. That she needed him in her life the way he needed her.

Instead, she picked Allen and her promotion.

"I was kidding myself," he muttered. Once again, he'd failed to see the truth right in his face.

"Kidding yourself about what?"

That she felt the same way he did. Whenever he thought about how he raced to her office, like an eager little puppy ready to share his feelings, he wanted to kick himself. "Nothing."

He could feel Mike's eyes studying him. "Wow. You've got it bad for her, don't you?" he said a few moments later.

"Worse than bad," Grant replied, washing a hand over his features. He'd never felt this intensely about a woman in his entire life. She'd gotten inside his head and under his skin. Dominated his thoughts to the point of utter distraction. He missed her smile, her warmth, her flawed interior. He must have picked up the phone a half-dozen times to call her only to come to his senses at the last minute.

"You'd think I'd know better," he said aloud. "The fact she shoved 'cease and desist' notes under my door should have been enough of a warning to stay far, far away."

"So what hooked you?"

"My own idiocy." Picking up his fork, he twirled his cocktail napkin, each turn causing the paper to bunch and tear. "Do you remember the doll Nicole used to keep on her bed? The one with the frilly blue dress?"

"You mean the one you ruined with Magic Marker?"

In spite of his bad mood, a corner of Grant's mouth twitched upward. "I prefer the word *enhance,* thank you very much. Sophie reminds me of her. On the outside, she's all pretty and polished, but underneath she's got lines and scars like everyone else." *I used to wish I could fly....*

"Maybe more," he added in a voice almost too low to be heard over the crowd. "She thinks she has to be this perfect employee. Like she's afraid if the world sees the real Sophie, she'll be some kind of failure. I wish she could see those flaws are what I love about her."

He paused. Love? Having never made such a declaration before to anyone besides family, he was shocked how easily the word slid off his tongue. Yeah, he loved Sophie. Had since that day they visited Nate. Fat lot of good it did him now.

Across the table, Mike continued studying him. Instead of his usual no-nonsense business expression, however, he wore a strange, almost contemplative expression. "Fear of failure can be a pretty strong motivator," he said after a moment. He raised his beer again. "Trust me, I know."

"I suppose." But Sophie, Grant hoped would be different. That she'd want to be different.

Why? a voice asked. Because he'd gotten her into his bed and convinced her to sleep in a few mornings? Talk about misplaced faith. No one was that good a renovator. Not even him.

He gave the fork another twist. "You want to hear ironic? When I called her on her behavior, she actually accused me of being the frightened one."

Mike looked to his pasta carbonara.

"You've got to be kidding me. Don't tell me you agree with her."

"I didn't say that."

He didn't have to. Annoyed, Grant tossed his fork down. It landed on his plate with a loud clank. "I can't believe this. You're both crazy."

Are they? a little voice in the back of his head

asked, much to his irritation. *Where there's smoke there's fire.*

"If I'm so afraid," he said, challenging Mike and the voice, "why'd I take the job with St. Pierre?"

Again, Mike said nothing, apparently still fascinated by his pasta. "I don't know. Why did you?"

To avoid Sophie. The thought hit him like a ton of bricks. He'd been running away. "I thought you were glad I took the job."

"I am. I'm just wondering what made you reverse your position after two years hiding from anything remotely close to success."

This time Grant was the one staring at his food. "What can I say? I decided it was time to move on. You're the one who told me I had to stop blaming myself for what happened to Nate."

"Have you?"

No. Not really. Deep in his heart the fear he would become the man from the emergency room window still lurked. He was beginning to wonder if he would ever truly outrun him. Maybe if he had more in his life besides a job. Like Sophie.

An unreadable expression crossed Mike's face, one Grant had never seen before. "Look, I'm all for you finally letting go of your guilt. If you really are. If you aren't accepting one painful reality to avoid another."

Grant arched a brow. "No offense, but you sound like one of those afternoon television psychiatrists."

Mike shrugged. "I just want you to be happy, little brother, and you haven't been. Not in a long time. I'd blame Nate, but I'm not sure you were happy before that."

He'd been too busy to be happy, thought Grant. And then Nate had his heart attack and he'd been too guilty. Too scared.

Except for the week he spent with Sophie. If every week was like that week, he'd be over the moon.

Unfortunately, that ship had sailed and he'd helped launch it.

"You should talk to her," Mike said.

"Sophie?"

"No, the waitress. Yes, Sophie. It's obvious

you're still nuts about her. Maybe she misses you, too."

Grant shook his head. "She made her choice."

"You sure? Like I said, fear makes people behave in weird ways. Some run away from work, others bury themselves with it. And some, didn't know their lives could have more than what they already have."

For the first time, Grant heard regret in his brother's voice. Perhaps the Templeton way hadn't been as kind to his older brother as he thought. Could he have misread the signs with Sophie, as well?

"You'll never know unless you try," Mike told him.

What do you know? Turns out his brother might actually have useful insight after all. "Maybe you aren't such a hard-hearted windbag after all," he teased.

If he'd underestimated his brother, had he underestimated Sophie, too?

"Besides," his brother added, signaling the waitress. "Since when did a Templeton not go after what he wanted?"

Grant sat back. Dammit if his brother wasn't right. Time he stopped running from things, and head toward them.

Gotta grab it. Otherwise you'll miss out.

The damn words were like a cadence the entire way home. *Gotta grab it. Gotta grab it.* Over and over until by the time Sophie reached her living room she wanted to scream, "I get it! The coat was Grant!"

Okay, she'd let something special slip through her fingers. She'd mistakenly believed that she had to stay a certain course and that any detour was wrong. Her psyche didn't need to beat it into her head. Besides, Grant was in Philadelphia. It wasn't as though she could do anything with the lesson except log it for next time.

If there was a next time. Grant really was like the coat. One of a kind and unlikely to be repeated.

She flopped on her sofa, not caring if she was sweaty and disheveled. Grant had liked her that way. He'd wanted the Sophie with the flaws. A person she didn't think anyone could want.

And she loved him. Of all the realizations to hit, that hit the hardest. Sure, she'd said things like loved and lost, but it dawned on her that she really loved him. Like forever, I-don't-care-if-you're-twenty-nine-or-ninety-nine love.

Oh, man, she was the biggest idiot on the face of the earth. Soon to be the loneliest idiot on the earth. As if she could be any lonelier. She already missed Grant like she missed breathing.

Somewhere in the middle of her pity party, she heard the sound of footsteps on the stairs and the sound of a door closing. Her heart stopped. It was Saturday. Grant was home.

Sophie sat up. When she was a kid, did she feel sorry for herself or did she pull herself up and get away from Pond Street? Exactly. So why was she lying around feeling sorry for herself now?

In a flash, she was on her feet and heading to Grant's door. He was going to listen to her and hear her out whether he liked it or not.

Clearing the last few steps, she ran to his door and knocked.

Her shoulders slumped. No answer. Same as the first time she knocked.

Face it. Grant wasn't home. She'd been so certain when the realization hit, she heard the footsteps but didn't think about the fact they might not be Grant's. She sank to the floor. What now? Camp out until he got home? What if he was on a date?

Oh, God, what if he showed up with some pretty young thing and saw her sitting here by his door like some lonely stalker?

Maybe this was a bad idea. The best thing would be to go downstairs and think out a plan of action.

No. Plans are what got her in trouble in the first place. She was going to sit right here and wait. Though wasn't that in itself a plan?

The sound of knocking interrupted her internal debate. Took her a moment, but she realized the pounding came from her apartment. Pushing herself back to her feet, she walked to the top of the stairway.

Grant stood at the bottom.

Sophie's breath caught. He looked as handsome as ever, his shoulders broad and strong. Shoulders Sophie knew now were perfect for leaning against. And his eyes, caramel and sparkling with surprise. How had she thought her world would be all right without those eyes?

"The coat was gone," she said, coming down a few steps.

"What?"

"The coat was gone," she repeated. As statements went, she could have done better, but her brain was too scared to think of anything but grabbing hold of what she really wanted. "I went back to the flea market and someone else had bought it. The vendor told me you have to move fast if you see something or risk losing out. Especially if you see something you really, really want."

He looked at her, confused. "What are you talking about?"

"I didn't know," she told him, risking another step closer, "because I didn't realize then what I know now.

"See, you're the coat. Took me a long time and a whole lot of wasted shuttles to Boston before I understood what I really and truly needed. And it's not being managing director. I thought when I got the job, I'd feel more secure. Safe. I don't."

"Wait, back up. You got the job?"

That's right, he didn't know. She nodded.

"Congratulations."

"Don't bother. The job is lonely. I spend all my days on the road. I haven't slept in my own bed for more than two nights since I took the job. Even when I do sleep at home, it's not the same."

"I know what you mean."

She glanced up through her lashes. Her vision was blurring. "I bought this co-op because I wanted the home I never had. Thing is, the only time it really felt like a home was that one week we were together. I want that back, Grant. I want to come home and share my day with you, have coffee in the morning and listen to you tease me about all the frozen pizza I've stored in the freezer. I want to spend my weekends procrastinating over my to-do list and soaking in your big tub while you complain about modern design."

Grant blinked. His caramel-colored eyes glistened, even though there was no sunlight. "Do you mean that?"

"Uh-huh. I was an idiot for not realizing sooner. Truth is, it doesn't matter how much younger you are than me or what you do, or what I do. Only thing that matters is being with you. I love you, Grant Templeton. I don't know how it happened or why or what it means to you, but I love you. And I'd like us to have a second chance. Please."

She took another step. "I don't want to lose you."

Unless she already had. His silence was beginning to scare her. Sophie's heart began to crumple. Too little, too late. She'd taken too long to realize what she had.

"You were right—no good ever comes out of tunnel vision. If you're willing to give us a second chance, I swear I'll remember and never—"

That's as far as she got because Grant leaped up the last few stairs and pulled her tight, his mouth claiming hers in one swift movement. They stumbled sideways, arms wrapped around one another, until they found the wall. There they grasped and clung to one another, neither able to get close enough. It was a kiss of mutual possession, of mutual need, of mutual surrender.

Eventually Grant broke away to breathe and Sophie found herself looking into hooded eyes that glowed with an emotion she was too nervous to name. She needed to hear the words said aloud.

"I love you, too, Sophie. That's why I was banging on your door. I was so focused on not repeating my mistakes, I made the same ones again. I forgot to fight for the person I cared about."

She pressed her fingers to his lips. "Grant…"

"No, no, let me say this." He kissed her fingertips. "I should never have walked away from you that night. I should have grabbed you and told you what I was feeling then and there. You were right, it was my ego. And fear."

"We were both scared, Grant. I still am," she admitted, a shiver running down her spine.

"Me, too. But I'm not avoiding it anymore."

He smiled and Sophie warmed from the inside out. "And I'm going to take the risk," she said, sealing the promise with a long intimate kiss.

Grant brushed his nose against hers. "I really do love you, Sophie Messina. I think I have from the second you accused me of stealing your water."

"I promise I'll never accuse you of that again."

"Hope not, since I plan to be sharing that water with you."

He kissed her again. Gentler this time, with a promise of all the time in the world. Sophie lost herself in the moment, so much so she gasped when she felt her feet leave the ground.

"What are you doing?" she asked, only to realize Grant had swept her in his arms.

"Shh. I'm going for a romantic gesture. Don't ruin the moment."

"Sorry," she whispered. "Carry on." She laid her hand on his shoulder, amazed at how happy she was. Happier than she could ever remember. She really had come a long way from Pond Street after all, hadn't she? Of course, they still had a lot of issues to deal with. His job in Philadelphia. Her job in New York. Their age difference. What if he wanted kids? Not that she wouldn't mind carrying Grant's child. In fact, the thought actually made her heart jump a little.

"Sophie." Grant was looking down at her and reading her thoughts. He pressed a gentle kiss to her forehead. "We'll figure it out as we go."

Seeing the love reflected in his eyes, Sophie suddenly realized that, yes, they would. Closing her eyes, she rested her cheek against his heart, and let the man she loved carry her home.

EPILOGUE

"ARE you sure you want to do this?" Grant asked.

Sophie nodded. She sat on the kitchen counter, where Grant had dropped her following his arrival home. Her stocking feet swung shoeless against the cabinet. She'd left her shoes somewhere along the way; it was so hard to keep track when you're being carried and kissed senseless at the same time. Absence did make the heart grow fonder after all.

Although they weren't spending all that much time apart anymore, were they? "We don't have to do this," Grant continued. "You still have time to think about it."

"Nope. I have thought about it, and I love everything. Besides, I'm done with making plans, remember?"

"Really? I seem to recall a new master plan?"

Sophie rolled her eyes. He would tease her

about that. A couple of weeks after their reunion, she'd decided that spending her weeknights in different hotel rooms was not satisfactory, particularly when Twamley Greenwood had an office in Philadelphia. And so, amid much teasing from Grant she embarked on creating a new master plan. This one had her marching into Allen Breckinridge's office and demanding a transfer. Turns out, Allen, king of the demands, actually responded to ones made of him, as well. Either that or Sophie really was his go-to gal because after some initial grumbling, he capitulated. Now, instead of jetting back and forth to Boston, she jetted back and forth to Philadelphia, and spent many more nights wrapped in peppermint-scented bliss.

"Just get the sledgehammer," she ordered him.

"As you wish." Opening the pantry door a little wider, he picked up the hammer and headed inside, only to poke his head out again. "You know that designwise, we are breaking all sorts of rules."

"Stop it. This was your idea."

"Yes," he said with a sigh. "It was, wasn't it?"

He disappeared into the pantry. A few moments later, Sophie heard a giant bang, followed by another, and then a loud crack.

"Did you break through?" she called out. Eager to see, she hopped down off the counter.

"Careful, there's splinters on the floor," Grant cautioned her when she peeked through the doorway. He was covered with white dust, and peeling away bits of plaster. "There you go," he said, grabbing a flashlight. "One secret passage."

Sophie followed the flashlight beam. Faintly, through the hole, she could make out the shape of the stairs. They were rickety and old, but they were intact.

"With a little bit of work, we'll have a real working staircase," Grant said, his smile glowing white in the dark space. "Our apartments will officially be connected."

Sophie smiled. "The way they should be," she told him. "The way they should be."

* * * * *

Mills & Boon® Large Print

December 2012

CONTRACT WITH CONSEQUENCES
Miranda Lee

THE SHEIKH'S LAST GAMBLE
Trish Morey

THE MAN SHE SHOULDN'T CRAVE
Lucy Ellis

THE GIRL HE'D OVERLOOKED
Cathy Williams

MR RIGHT, NEXT DOOR!
Barbara Wallace

THE COWBOY COMES HOME
Patricia Thayer

THE RANCHER'S HOUSEKEEPER
Rebecca Winters

HER OUTBACK RESCUER
Marion Lennox

A TAINTED BEAUTY
Sharon Kendrick

ONE NIGHT WITH THE ENEMY
Abby Green

THE DANGEROUS JACOB WILDE
Sandra Marton